Cedar Creek
Christmas at Cedar Creek
Snowstorm at Cedar Creek

Pine Harbor
Allison's Pine Harbor Summer
Evelyn's Pine Harbor Autumn
Lydia's Pine Harbor Christmas

Holiday House
The Christmas Cabin
The Winter Lodge
The Lighthouse
The Christmas Castle
The Beach House
The Christmas Tree Inn
The Holiday Hideaway

Highland Passage
Highland Passage
Knight Errant
Lost Bride

Highland Soldiers

The Enemy
The Betrayal
The Return
The Wanderer

Highland Vow

American Hearts

Secret Hearts
Runaway Hearts
Forbidden Hearts

For more information, visit jljarvis.com.

THE BEACH HOUSE

THE BEACH HOUSE

A HOLIDAY HOUSE NOVEL

J.L. JARVIS

BOOKBINDER PRESS

THE BEACH HOUSE
A Holiday House Novel

Published by Bookbinder Press
bookbinderpress.com

ISBN 978-1-942767-23-7 (trade paperback)
ISBN 978-1-942767-17-6 (paperback)
ISBN 978-1-942767-16-9 (ebook)

ONE

"I'll take it."

Wanda Humphrey peered over her glasses. "But you haven't seen it yet."

From her seat on the opposite side of the desk, Jess Pelletier glanced at the computer screen filled with real estate listings. "Is there anything else there in my budget that you haven't shown me?"

"Well, not really, but... "

With a shrug, Jess repeated, "I'll take it."

Mrs. Humphrey studied Jess for a moment. "Well, if you're sure."

Jess nodded firmly. "I am."

"Okay. Then I'll need to draw up the lease. There's a diner a few doors down. Why don't you go have some lunch, and I'll bring you the lease to sign when it's ready?"

Jess brightened. "Sounds perfect."

She paused when she reached the door, but before she could ask, Mrs. Humphrey said, "To your left, three doors down, on this side of the street."

Jess flashed a smile and left the storefront real estate office. She drew in a deep breath of sea air and headed down the sidewalk, passing the old storefronts that lined the main street of Applecross Cove. A few cars drove by, obstructing her view, then the road cleared to reveal the harbor. The low-hanging branches of pines reached out, framing the view where the water opened up to the sea.

Most of the old fishermen's huts were long gone, having given way to cedar-shingled seafood shacks. The sides of the small cottages were decked with faded buoys and old wooden rounded-end lobster traps whose hand-knitted heads hung in shreds. A few boats and sloops bobbed in the sparkling water ahead.

Jess paused outside the diner to take it all in. This would be her new home.

After weathering more than a century as a hardworking fishing village, Applecross Cove had retained much of its original character. The little town had gone through some hard times, which may have protected it from so-called modern improvements by real estate developers that had marred some coastal towns. But Applecross Cove's buildings stood as noble monuments to an era gone by. In recent years, some of the old stores had been repurposed into quaint touristy shops selling pottery, souvenirs, gifts, and fresh homemade fudge. But within the town's stunning setting and its horseshoe-shaped harbor was its heartbeat. The crabbers and trawlers had persevered, bringing Applecross Cove to its current state of proud, unspoiled charm. For Applecross Cove was a working harbor, and if its residents had anything to say about it, it would always be so. Too far-flung and rustic to be overrun by summer tourists, the town tolerated a modest increase in summer population for the money it brought to the local economy. But now it was spring, and it was coming to life as newly green trees swayed and cowered to the chilly winds coming in from the sea, while the crocuses shivered below.

Three doors down, as Mrs. Humphrey had told her, Jess found the diner. In all of its chrome-and-neon glory, it was a shining example of as much modernization as the town had allowed. Between the looks of the place and the weathered vessels that peppered the harbor, Jess half expected to be met with a room full of crusty, pipe-smoking sailors in matching yellow rain slickers and hats. Instead, she found a diner full of ordinary people in the same sort of outdoor clothing she might find in a city coffee shop. This diner was especially crowded, which was to be expected since it was barely past noon.

A waitress in a T-shirt and corduroy jeans walked by with plates stacked up her arm. She tilted her ponytailed head toward a small table by the front window. Taking that as an invitation, Jess walked to it and sat down.

Moments later, the waitress appeared. "Something to drink?"

"Coffee, please."

As quickly as she'd arrived, the young woman was gone.

Jess looked at the window and studied the rivulets of condensation dripping down the edge of the glass, and she took in the musical murmurs and clinks that hovered in the warm air as unhurried diners talked over their meals.

Living here was going to be perfect.

WEEKS BEFORE, Jess had gotten the call to go meet with a team from human resources in a conference room of the company where she worked as a marketing analyst. She'd been good at her job, which had always confounded her. Why couldn't she have been good at something she loved? She supposed she should have considered it a favor when, in their latest quarterly massacre, the company had announced its corporate earnings along with a new batch of layoffs. She'd seen it all happen before—just not to her.

She was called into a room where a half dozen suits were sitting around a conference table.

The woman in the center spoke first. "As we announced in our town hall meeting..."

I've always liked that description—a corporate town hall meeting. It sounds like referring to a dog fight as a puppy playdate.

"We've undergone an assessment of our product and geographic portfolio. Forecasts point to strong organic revenue."

I know. Because I worked on those forecasts.

"With our relentless commitment to automation well underway, we've begun the next phase of our corporate restructuring."

Corporate restructuring. That's kind of like calling a guillotine a body part relocation facilitator.

"We've identified four areas of core competency, one of which is your group. Our IT group has already shifted to the new paradigm as we deepen our exploration of global outsourcing."

So... you've laid off the tech team and hired cheap third-world labor.

"And now we turn to marketing. There are a lot of

rumors flying around, so we're going to disambiguate those. We're offering you an independence opportunity outside of the purview of our corporate culture and remuneration construct."

Huh? "You're laying me off?"

"Yes." She slid a folder across the table. "Let's walk through your severance package."

Jess gave the impression of listening as a rush of thoughts and sensations overwhelmed her senses. By the time they were finished, she felt numb and a little light-headed as two security guards escorted her out of the building, but not past her coworkers. That was not a surprise. During restructuring—a corporate euphemism that fooled no one ever—people just disappeared through an alternate exit. The remaining employees never witnessed the shocked faces and tears of those, who after tireless sacrifices—long hours worked, missed school concerts and sporting events— were rewarded with a severance package and a life torn apart. Jess hadn't been able to say goodbye to the people she'd worked with for years. They had helped one another through work challenges and had commiserated under the thumb of a couple of bosses, the kind who always got promoted because people were tools of production. Over lunch, she and her coworkers had shared news of blind dates, sick children, and parents. Theirs was a bond that made workplaces human. So it was fitting for the final corporate act to sever that bond with a swift, sharp blow.

Jess and her security experts arrived at the exit. Outside, it was snowing. She reflexively reached for her keys then remembered she'd turned them in at the meeting. Of course they would be keeping her company car. Not to worry, they'd arranged for a car service to drive her home. There was a line of cars waiting. She got in the first one. She could come back on Friday to collect her desk contents.

The ride home felt longer than it usually did, probably because when she was driving, she had more control. But control was a thing of the past. Jess's future was a blank slate. The prospect terrified her, but she held it together.

She walked through her front door, typed and emailed her thirty-day notice to her landlord, then drank a bottle of wine. She could sleep in the next morning.

TWO

THE HANGING BELL rang as a customer opened the door to the diner. The server set down a thick porcelain mug of coffee, took her order, and vanished again.

Jess had made the move quickly. There she was, three weeks to the day after being laid off, sitting in a café and beginning a new life, or at least taking a break from the one she had known. Halfway through her toasted BLT sandwich, her phone rang. When she saw it was her mother, she tapped her screen to answer. "Yes, Mom, I made it."

Adam. That didn't take long. Her stomach sank—a feeling she'd grown accustomed to lately. "No, I haven't heard from him. Why would I? It's over." She took a sip of her coffee while keeping the phone pressed against her ear.

Her mother would not let it go. "What's Adam going to do?"

"I don't know. We're not engaged anymore, so that's not my problem."

Moments passed as she listened to her mother's latest news. Jess tried not to be troubled by the fact that her mother had more going on in her life than she did. But as the conversation returned to Jess's move, her spirits lifted. "So anyway, I found a place. In fact, I'm about to sign a lease. Yeah, I know. No, I didn't waste any time." *And I'm happy about it, unlike you.* "Well, let me get settled first, then you can come see it." She grinned and glanced up to find a man looking down at her... a very good-looking man. She lowered her eyes, feeling a little unsettled. "Excuse me, Mom." She lifted her eyes back up. He was tall with straight brown hair barely long enough to be tousled. His broad shoulders put the seams of his navy fleece jacket to the test. And he was staring with unreadable deep-set blue eyes.

The waitress stopped in her tracks and stared at him. He was blocking her way.

"Oh, I'm sorry." He was so kind and sincere that the woman's eyes softened. He slipped into the seat opposite Jess uninvited.

"Mom, I'll call you back." She ended the call with her mother and put her phone down on the table. With her brow furrowed and mouth slightly agape, she took in the sight of the stranger who had just invaded her space.

Before she could speak, he asked, "Miss Pelletier?"

Her eyebrows lifted in surprise. "Yes."

He extended his hand with an easy charm. "Mark Breton." He lifted a file folder. "My aunt sent me here with the lease."

Jess's eyebrows drew together. Her eyebrows were going to be sore tomorrow. She wondered how many calories brow-lifting burned.

"Wanda Humphrey. Humphrey Real Estate?" He peered at her inquisitively. "I'm sorry. She said you were just in her office."

"I was. But she said she'd be coming."

A look of recognition dawned on his face as he leaned over. "Oh. Sorry," he said quietly.

Jess wondered what he was sorry for, other than the awkward tension between them. Or maybe she was the only one who felt that. She wasn't feeling too warmly toward men these days.

Mark put his hands on the file folder he'd set on the table. "She does this sometimes."

Jess realized she was frowning again.

He nodded. "I take it you're single."

Feeling skeptical and a little on guard, Jess leaned back and reflexively glanced toward the exit. As attractive as Mark was—and he was very attractive—

things were taking a turn from awkward to weird. Jess wasn't the sort of girl who sat down in diners and had handsome men fall at her feet—or sit at her table.

Jess had been cursed with dark-brown hair, and in her experience, that sort of thing only happened to blondes. She'd argued about that with her friends who were blonde, but they were just being nice by disagreeing. She was reminded of the world's preference for blondes every time she turned on her favorite news channel. A newscaster might start out as a brunette, but by the time the makeup and hair crews were done with her, she would be a blonde. It began benignly enough with some subtle highlights, but weeks later, all that remained of the original woman were her roots. Jess had seen it too many times. It was sad and a little disturbing. But she was stronger than that. She had kept her color and all of the invisibility that came with it.

Mark held up his palms defensively. "That didn't come out right. I'm not asking for me."

Jess opened her mouth to protest but decided to save time and just leave. She would stop by Wanda's and straighten things out. But before she could push back from the table, Mark hastened to add, "It's my aunt. She... it's... what she does."

Jess stared at him. "What?" She couldn't help but

wonder if everyone in Applecross Cove was just a little bit off.

He shook his head and gave her an embarrassed smile that even Jess had to admit was disarming. "She fixes me up—or she tries. I'm single. Happily so, I assure you. This isn't coming from me. But I can't seem to dissuade Aunt Wanda from the notion that two single young people should be, well, paired off."

Jess shook her head. "Well that's just—"

"Crazy? I know. But sometimes she gets it into her head. She must like you. So, lucky you, here I am."

Jess leaned back, unsure of whether to say thank you or just ignore the whole thing.

While she decided, Mark continued talking. "She means well, but don't worry. I promise you this will be a completely platonic real estate transaction." He followed that statement with an expression of embarrassed amusement she couldn't help but return.

Jess relaxed. "I'm sure she just wants the best for you."

He raised his hands and gestured toward Jess.

"Oh," she quickly added. "I didn't mean... I'm not that. Obviously. I just meant... "

"I know what you meant." He smiled, and she smiled, and silence wedged itself between them.

Jess broke the spell first. "So, that's settled. Aunt Wanda's devious plot has been foiled. So..."

"Mark."

Jess realized he had misunderstood. "No, I remembered your name, I was just... it's a bad habit... saying so." *When I'm nervous.*

Mark's eyebrows drew together, and he gave a nod. "Oh, right. To fill in awkward silence. Not that this is awkward. Well, it wasn't until I made it so."

Jess shook her head, but she couldn't find the words to reassure him when it was precisely that. Awkward.

He slowly blinked then lifted his eyes to meet hers with a crooked, self-deprecating smile on his lips. "You can see why I'm single."

Well, actually, no, not really. His messy nut-brown hair was clearly incapable of landing in an unflattering arrangement. Beneath it was a face with strong but irregular features. Then there were the shoulders, broad and strong—but not in a steroidal, hours-at-the-gym sort of way. They had more of a manly hoist-the-yardarm appearance that was almost too virile to resist.

She took a moment to ponder the image then decided his masculine presence more than made up for his slightly lumbering manner. But it was those blue eyes in the midst of it all that made her lose track of her own train of thought. Not that she was interested in him in *that* way. She was simply acknowledging facts. He just happened to resemble a Renaissance statue... with clothes. And that got her wondering if she could, in fact, find him attractive.

"Yeah." She glanced up with the sudden realization that her mind had been wandering and she'd answered out loud. "I mean no! I can't see why you're single. I assume that you're single by choice, same as me." *Not because your fiancé turned out to be spineless and irresponsible and more or less ruined your life.*

His eyes sparkled with amusement.

Jess couldn't seem to stop herself. "Life's so much easier, isn't it? Without complications?" *Or deep disappointment, betrayed trust, and a broken heart.*

"We've definitely dodged a bullet there."

She swiped a hand across her forehead. "No kidding! Phew!" *Jess, stop talking now before you say something too honest.*

He leaned on his elbows. "But I'm not completely opposed to the concept of friendship."

When his cobalt eyes settled on hers, her heart skipped a beat. Jess managed a shrug. "Well, yeah. Friends are good. I actually have one or two."

"But none here in town?"

She hesitated. "No. Not yet." Only then did it sink in that she was alone—truly, completely, entirely alone. The whole move had been an impulse, one that had just caught up with her. In an effort to escape from her heartache and reminders thereof, she had isolated herself in a small town so far north, she was practically in Canada. Not that that was a bad thing. She loved Canada. But she was a Mainer and always would be. Besides, everyone she knew and could count on was still within driving distance, just not shopping or lunch distance. But that was what she had wanted—time alone, time to figure out life.

At some point in her musings, a cup of coffee appeared before Mark. He took a sip. "Oh, I'm sorry. Please don't let me interrupt your lunch."

She had half of a BLT left, so she took a bite and felt a blob of tomato and mayo land on her chin.

He politely ignored her desperate grab for a napkin and continued to talk as though nothing had happened. "I don't want to impose, but if you need someone local —a friend—I'd be happy to stand in until you can do better." An easy smile lit his face as he reached into his pocket, pulled out a business card, and handed it to her.

She took it, convinced she had undoubtedly brought on his gesture of pity with the lost-puppy feeling that must have found its way onto her face.

As she stared at the card, he said, "Don't worry. We've got a good recycling program."

Jess scanned the card then let out a light laugh. "No, I'll keep it. It'll come in handy if I have a real estate emergency." She flipped her hair back over her shoulder then inwardly groaned. *A real estate emergency? A hair flip? What am I doing?* Not flirting. Sure, the guy was well-groomed and personable.

She inwardly laughed at herself. Fine, he was handsome. There was nothing wrong with admitting that. It was perfectly normal to find a man attractive, just like it was perfectly normal to stand in front of one of those Renaissance paintings of massively muscular men who happened to be naked and stare at them until a crowd gathered because you were blocking their view. No, that never happened.

He shrugged. "It could happen."

Jess's eyes opened wide. *What? Don't tell me I said that out loud.*

"A real estate emergency," he added. "It could happen."

She nodded and managed a nervous smile.

He laughed, a light and easy sound. It put her at ease, so much so that she didn't blink an eye as the waitress cleared her plate from the table. It may as well have disappeared.

Mark took one last sip from his coffee and set it aside. With a satisfied sigh—the guy clearly liked coffee —he opened the file folder containing the lease that Jess had nearly forgotten about. He pulled out some papers and set them on the table. "It's been used as a holiday rental, but my aunt got tired of managing the bookings."

"Oh. She didn't mention that she'd be my landlord."

"Yeah. But if anything goes wrong, just call me. It'll save a step in the process." He smiled. "You could call her, but she'd just turn around and call me. So you might want to keep that card after all. My number's on it." He proceeded to go over the terms of the lease, pointing at each paragraph with a cheap ballpoint pen that he held in his large working-man hand.

When he was finished, Jess signed it.

Mark slid out of his seat and excused himself. "Be right back."

Jess gazed out at the main street of the town that was her new home. She'd done it. She'd been laid off, moved out of her apartment, and rented a cottage for six months with a month-to-month option after that.

Mark soon returned and put on his jacket. "Are you parked at the office?"

"Yes."

"Me too. I'll walk you back, and you can follow me to the apartment."

"You don't have to do that."

But when he extended his arm toward the door, she followed his cue and went first. The April air smelled of the sea and fresh flowers.

"We like to be there to hand clients the key. And to be honest, it also gives us a chance for a last-minute assessment of the property's condition when tenants take possession."

"Just before I start having wild parties and trashing the place?"

His eyes sparkled. "Yeah. You and your one or two out-of-town friends."

"Exactly." As she laughed, her eyes met his, and she made a decision. If they were going to be friends, she would have to get over those piercing blue eyes.

THREE

Jess followed Mark's pickup onto a gravel driveway that wound gently down a curved, tree-lined slope until the sea appeared. Its deep-blue surface was roughened by waves, and as they struck the rocky coastline, a white spray rose to the pale-blue sky, which was interrupted only by an occasional cotton-puff cloud. Tall, scattered pines stood guard by a small silver-shingled cottage that looked out at the water.

Mark was already leaning against his truck door by the time Jess caught her breath and got out of her car. "Well, what do you think? Wait, come here first." He waved for her to follow as he walked around to the deck, where two white-painted Adirondack chairs sat facing the water.

Jess stood on the deck and took in the view of the ocean, which was skirted by cottages along the coastline in either direction. Emotion surged up with no warning, and she swallowed. The vastness, the peace, and the power of the sea may as well have washed over her, for it rendered her unable to move for a moment. By the time she regained enough control to look at Mark, she was met with a look of gentle understanding. There was no way he could have known how she felt, let alone what had led her to that point, but she felt a sympathetic silence from him as he stood quietly by.

She turned to him and caught a glimpse of wistfulness in his eyes, but they quickly brightened. "Come on. I'll show you the inside. Let's go back around so you can take in the grand entrance."

She'd been so entranced by the sea view that she'd failed to notice the daffodils and hyacinths surrounding the cottage. "Oh, how pretty!"

Mark's eyes glimmered. "The tulips will come up soon, as will the lupines. All summer, there's something new blooming. Aunt Wanda wanted an English country garden. It's not quite that, but I hope it'll do."

They stood and admired the garden for a moment, then Jess felt a sudden dismay.

Mark turned to her. "What's the matter? Oh, you're not allergic, are you?"

Jess peered at him. "No."

His forehead crinkled in confusion. "You hate flowers?"

She looked straight at him. "Gardens like this don't happen by chance."

"So I've heard," he said wryly.

"I love it! All the flowers, the shape of the beds. It's almost like a storybook. But if it's left to me... well, it's only a matter of time. I try. I follow directions and do all the right things, but any plant I've ever had anything to do with has withered and died."

"Oh." His eyebrows drew together as he gave a slight nod, then his eyes swept along the full length of the flower bed before them.

She tried not to look hopeless. "If I had some instructions, I could try. There must be a YouTube video on it." She looked up to find him looking at her with something between horror and amusement, or maybe it was more of a scoff.

As if catching himself, he assumed a more patient expression. "Don't worry. The landscaping's included."

"It is? I don't remember anything about that in the lease." She started to unfold the papers, but he put his hand on hers to stop her, which it certainly did. In fact, she nearly forgot what they'd been talking about.

"It is now." He smiled, but there was something subtly patronizing about it that irked her a little less subtly.

"But landscaping's not cheap. Shouldn't you check with your aunt?"

"I don't need to. Her landscaper says he'll take care of it." His mouth turned up at one corner. "That would be me."

"You did this? But it's gorgeous!" A second later, she realized that her mouth was agape, which must have looked really pretty.

Mark acknowledged the compliment with a modest nod and moved on. "So, that's settled. I'll stop by once a week or two. So don't mind me if you look out the window and see me in your flower beds."

Jess wouldn't have minded finding him in any of her beds, but she managed to keep that thought to herself. "So if you're shoveling dirt, I shouldn't assume that you're burying a body?"

He glanced sideways at her. "I didn't say that." *Damn that charming manner of his.* "I'm kidding!"

"I was hoping..." She began to doubt her own sense of humor since she'd sent the conversation down this path—the garden path.

He gave her an admonishing look. "You started it, so blame yourself."

"Oh, I do."

He laughed. "If I return to find a new security system installed, I'll know we don't share the same brand of humor."

"It's not a name brand." Jess glanced up into those gentle blue eyes and found it hard to maintain her smirk.

"Let's call it a boutique brand. Makes it sound classier."

She couldn't seem to stop smiling, but he was smiling right back.

Mark broke the spell. "I think it's time for the grand tour." He led the way up to the door, opened it, then turned and held the keys out for her. "After you.

"So, here we are. Living room, dining room, kitchen." He grinned. "It's a short tour."

"I can see." The kitchen was neutral and neat, with white shaker cabinets to go with the white trim throughout the cottage. Cream granite countertops with light-brown variegations and stainless appliances completed the decor. A window stretched from the sink to the vaulted ceiling, bathing the kitchen in afternoon sunlight. On the opposite side was the island, which separated the kitchen from the living area. There, a wall of windows looked out past the deck and gave way to a view of the sea. Across from the kitchen was a bathroom. Sunlight poured in from a skylight onto a sleek white soaking tub.

"There's no shower," he said apologetically.

Jess shook her head. "I don't care. I just love it."

A queen-size bed took up most of the cozy bedroom and faced a small fireplace.

"It's just fake. It's electric," Mark explained. "But I thought it would lend the room atmosphere on a gray day, don't you think?"

Jess surveyed the room, stunned by how closely it fit what she'd wished for when she first thought of moving.

For the first time since she'd met him, he seemed insecure. "Is it okay? Aunt Wanda turned this over to me as a project. I did most of the work."

"You did this?"

He shrugged.

"A real estate tycoon, gardener, and contractor-designer?"

He nodded a little bashfully. "More of a handyman, really."

"Who are you?" She stared with wide eyes but then laughed. "'Cause it's a little freaky how everything is just so... perfect."

He beamed. "So you like it?"

"I do."

"Well, good. I'll leave you to get settled then." He started toward the door then turned back. "There's shopping down the road. We passed it on our way."

"I remember."

"And if there's anything else, you can call me or

flag me down." He motioned toward the right. "I live just over there—three doors down."

"Okay, thanks." Jess smiled and walked him to the door. He cast one more smile her way before getting into his car and driving away.

Jess turned and gazed at her new home. She had done it. She'd found the perfect retreat, with a perfectly distracting neighbor. *Three doors down?* She went to the window and searched for his cottage. Jess was surprised to see a silvery cedar cottage with white trim built into the hill in such a way that the entrance next to the driveway was on the second floor. Wrapped around the side facing the sea was a two-story deck, from which a path led down the hill to two flights of stairs trailing down to the beach. A large sailboat was docked there that had to belong to someone in this cluster of cottages since they all shared the same stretch of gravelly beach. They also shared the same driveway and parking area, as well as a small row of mailboxes resting on a weathered beam.

Jess's gaze traveled back to Mark's cottage. Mark Breton, realtor, gardener, handyman, and handsome man. Jess heaved a sigh.

Mr. Mark "I'm single" Breton, you'd better not mess with my head. This head's got plans, and they don't include you.

FOUR

JESS WOKE up in her new home and put the coffee on. While she waited, she gazed out the window and watched the waves catch the sun on their way to the rocks jutting defiantly out from the shore. She took in a deep breath. For a week, she'd risen and looked out her kitchen window, each day more convinced that she'd managed to find the perfect place to heal her heart and make sense of her life.

A movement caught her eye. There he was, Mark—her neighbor, real estate agent, gardener, and handyman—standing at the edge of the dock. Every day at about the same time, he was there. And every day, she was here at her window, looking at him. She let her gaze linger for a few moments as he stood, staring out at the sea. She wondered what he thought as he stood there and stared. Something in his posture and bearing gave it more weight than the simple joy Jess felt when she took in the view. But then there were moments when Mark almost appeared as though he might take a dive, clothes and all, and go swimming. But ten minutes later, he would turn and walk up to his cottage.

And she would watch him. "Girl, get a grip. One week alone, and you're staring at neighbors, not to mention talking to yourself." She turned and finished putting the dishes away, muttering, "No harm in looking."

A knock sounded at the front door, and she smiled and went to answer it. She swung the door open and faced a slightly shorter, thirty-year-older version of herself with straight, brown shoulder-length hair and a bright, winning grin. They hugged, then Jess took her mother's hand and led her inside.

"So you found it okay?"

"I did."

Jess stretched out her arms. "This is it."

"Very cozy," Kelly Pelletier said as she followed Jess for a quick look inside the bedroom and bathroom before continuing through the back door to the deck.

Jess grabbed two cups of coffee and sat with her mother on the deck, taking in the view. A salty breeze blew in from the sea.

Kelly broke the silence. "This would make a great vacation rental."

Jess patiently said, "Or a home. People live here all year-round."

"Well, I know that. And it would be perfect—if you were a whaler."

Here we go. Jess smiled. "The whaling industry kinda gave way to the industrial revolution, which I'm sure you'll remember." *From firsthand experience.*

Kelly narrowed her eyes as she took in the cottages lining the shore. "I suppose you could take up scrimshaw to pass the time on those cold winter nights."

"When I'm not going out with Moby Dick."

Kelly replied with disdain. "Moby Dick was a whale."

Jess's eyes twinkled. "Yeah, well, Moby Dick, whale—I'm sure I've dated at least one of each."

Kelly shot that admonishing look Jess knew so well. "How are you going to meet anyone here? I'm pretty sure that Captain Gregg ran off with Mrs. Muir."

Jess shook her fist. "Dammit! And he was the last man on earth." She thought for a moment. "Well, he wasn't really on earth, technically, was he?"

Kelly adjusted in her seat. "I don't mean to rush you..."

Jess mouthed the next word. *"But."* Then she

interrupted her mother before she could start. "Look, Mom, I've signed a lease, so you may as well save your breath."

Kelly heaved a sigh. "I just want you to be happy."

Jess smiled patiently. "I know. So good news: I am."

"And what about work?"

Jess's eyes lost their light. "I got laid off. Remember?"

"Well, I know. But you'll need something to live on while you're here."

"The rent here is cheaper than my old place, and I've got enough severance to last until I get my business on its feet."

Kelly's eyes opened in surprise. "Well, good for you, honey. But it's good to have something to slow down the leak."

Jess stared for a moment then nodded. "Mom, I'm good. Got my big-girl pants on. Making big-girl decisions." *Did that sound too acerbic?*

Her mother reacted with silence and that expression Jess had known since she'd spilled her first milk. The moment passed, and Kelly stood up. "Well, while I'm here, we may as well get some seafood. My treat."

A movement caught Jess's eye. Mark was walking past her cottage, which wasn't so odd. It was a five-minute walk into town, and he was headed that way.

Kelly followed her gaze. "Well, at least the scenery's lovely."

"Mom." Jess hooked her arm about her mother's and guided her away from the window, wincing as she thought that she and her mother might find the same man attractive.

Hours later, having barely survived lunch, Jess smiled and waved as her mother drove out of the driveway and headed back home for Bangor. *Thanks, Mom. I'd almost forgotten how much my life sucked.*

Jess went over to check her mailbox, which sat on a beam with a half dozen others. It was empty, as she'd expected. Her bills were almost entirely paperless, and she hadn't ordered anything to be delivered... yet. So she was well ensconced in her self-imposed therapeutic exile from what troubled her, which was mainly the world.

"Jess!"

She turned to find Mark ambling toward her. But of course, he was coming to check his own mail. *Why would he go out of his way to see me?* He pulled a few letters out of his mailbox and turned to her with a lazy smile and his usual laid-back attitude. She wasn't sure whether to admire or resent how comfortable he was in his own skin. But as skin went, not to mention his muscles and athletic frame, who wouldn't be comfortable with that?

She gave him a small smile. "Hi."

He closed his mailbox and walked toward her, coming to a stop a few feet away. "So, settled in?" He glanced toward the end of the driveway, where her mother had just pulled out onto the road. "Entertaining already?"

Their eyes locked, then Jess resorted to humor to ease her inner tension. "Yup. Wild party. Trashed the place."

He played right along. "Good. Glad to hear you're having fun here."

"Well, to be honest, that was my mother."

"Oh, good."

"Good, yes, for the most part. But fun?" She wrinkled her face. "Not exactly."

He tilted his head and studied her. "Oh?"

For a brief moment, she actually contemplated opening up, then she inwardly shuddered as she thought of how desperate she was for someone to talk to. *You barely know him. Sharing would undoubtedly keep it that way.* She sighed. "Long story." She squinted then realized it was probably not her most attractive expression. "Actually, it's not really so long. Just a story you don't need to hear. You know, boring family dynamics. You'd be forced, out of politeness, to look interested. It's too much to ask at this point in our, uh, friendship."

He was suppressing something. Whether it was laughter *with* her or *at* her was not easy to say. She would need to study him further. Did his twinkling eyes seem to reflect the sky or the sea?

"Sorry," she said.

His eyebrows drew together. "For what?"

"Sometimes I ramble." She waited for him to say something, like tell her that no, she didn't ramble. Contradicting her would be the polite thing to do.

But he nodded. "And say 'so.'"

Her eyes flitted downward. "Oh. Yeah. I do that too." *Wow, he gets me. Or he just has a good memory.*

"Have you found everything that you need?"

She nodded amiably.

"Stores? Gas station?"

She nodded again.

"The ocean?"

Jess lifted her eyebrows and pointed back over her shoulder. "Back there, right?"

He chuckled. "That's it." He held her gaze for a moment then turned toward the sea. "Well, good." He fixed his eyes back on her, which caught her unprepared every time. "Glad you're all settled." He held up his mail. "Got some reading to do." His eyes sparkled with mirth. "See you around."

Nice smile. One slightly crooked front tooth, so he's human. Jess almost missed her cue. "Yeah. Bye!"

She walked back to her cottage and closed the front door.

This is silly. He is so not my type. Jess was used to business-casual clothes that emitted an "I'm more business than casual" vibe. She hadn't seen him check his phone even once. *Does he even have one? He's got to. How else can he keep tabs on his life goals and action plan?*

She took a moment to ponder life without lists.

And I'm not myself around him. Or maybe she was. Maybe that was the big problem—the elephant in the room. She scowled. *I am not the elephant in the room! No, that's not it. I was right the first time. I'm not myself with him.* She rambled because she was unsure of herself around him. And it only got worse when he gazed at her with those eyes that were so blindingly blue that she couldn't look directly at them without solar eclipse glasses. *Dammit! I'm only human!*

With her face still contorted with confusion, Jess sank into an overstuffed chair.

FIVE

Jess sat on a bench overlooking the harbor, enjoying the feel of the moist breeze blowing in from the Atlantic. Her leather-bound journal lay in her lap, but she'd barely written a word. It felt too good to be there, taking in the vision of off-season life in Applecross Cove. Now and then, people passed by on the walking and jogging path that wound its way around the water's edge and through the wooded park by the library.

She started to mull over her business objectives and opened her journal to jot down some ideas. She had given herself a week to unpack and get settled. Now it was on to phase two. She had stumbled upon her small work-from-home business while doing a favor for a friend. What had begun as a simple website design had grown until she'd had to hire help to keep up with the work while she held down her regular full-time career.

When the layoff had hit at her regular job, she'd seen her side gig as a chance to take her life and career in a whole new direction. With a one-year target, she intended to build her business to a one-stop source for small businesses to go to for website design, social media marketing, and virtual assistant services. She still had her small pool of part-time freelancers to draw from, so with thoughtful planning, hard work, and maybe some luck, she would be poised to succeed. The first task was to upgrade her website's bandwidth capacity and overhaul the site to make it look cutting edge. She leaned over her journal and added ideas and tasks to her lengthening list.

"Jess! You look intense."

Jess peered up at the figure in front of her. He was backlit, but she knew that voice and that build before she put her hand to her forehead to shade her eyes. "Mark?"

His breathing was still deep from running. "May I join you?"

"Sure." She shrugged as though she didn't care, but her heart rate said otherwise.

He leaned back on the bench, catching his breath.

"Out for a jog?" *Brilliant, Jess. The guy's dressed in athletic gear, and he's panting. Since it isn't for you, then yeah, he's been running.*

"Yeah. I go for a walk or a run about this time each morning."

She nodded with interest as though that were breaking news and she hadn't seen him run past every morning at nine.

He fixed his eyes on the sea. "It's a little chilly yet for most people, but when the weather warms up, you'll enjoy that small private beach that we share with our neighbors."

"Oh, I don't swim."

His jaw dropped in absolute shock.

"How could you not like swimming?"

Here we go. She'd had this conversation before, more than once. "It's not so much that I don't like it. It's just that I can't. I never needed to, really."

He stared, and she offered a helpless shrug.

He studied her for another moment. "We'll have to fix that."

Jess smiled, neither agreeing nor rejecting the proposal. It was merely one of those things people said without actually meaning to follow through. But she still felt the need to explain. "I grew up in the city."

Mark studied her for a moment then glanced up as

a shadow passed overhead. The look on his face didn't bode well. Jess followed his gaze to the overcast sky.

Mark stood up. "We might want to head for home before the sky opens up. If we're lucky, we can make it there dry."

She wished she could share his optimism. "Luck isn't something I've had much of lately."

He looked intent, as though he were going to ask her about that statement. But the sky darkened, and a strong gust came out of nowhere. "Are you finished here?"

Jess's first instinct was to say no, but a few drops of rain fell, then a few more. "I am now." She hastily stashed her pen and journal in her jacket pocket, then she realized Mark had essentially offered to walk her home. *How gallant.* Of course, he was just being nice. In the short time she'd known him, she'd learned that much about him. Mark Breton was nice.

It started to sprinkle, and Mark looked up with a knowing grin.

They walked in silence as the rain grew steadier. "I can't remember the last time someone walked me home. Maybe high school?" She smiled, and he returned it politely, but then she wondered if she'd made it weird by implying the two of them had some sort of romance, which they clearly did not. Her self-doubts weren't helped by the wary look on his face.

There was no other way to describe his expression. Alert simply wasn't enough. He was either afraid she had romantic intentions, or he was concerned for her mental well-being. It was probably both.

"I live three doors past you, so it's not really out of my way."

Jess nodded until she resembled a bobblehead in the back of a car. "Well, anyway..." *Anyway what?*

He was looking as though he were waiting for another thought to follow. It wouldn't. Her mind was a blank, so... business as usual.

It started to pour.

Mark turned to her. "Are you up for a run?"

Jess opened her mouth but had no time to answer. Mark took hold of her hand, and they ran along a path that followed the curve of the cove, ending on the stony beach. He surveyed the hill leading up to their cottages. "Let's find some shelter." Mark led her down one of the docks to a yacht. He unfastened the cover and pulled it aside to reveal the door to the cabin. "Go in." He held the cover for her before following her into the cabin.

Once inside, Jess wrung her shoulder-length hair out then combed her fingers through the wet clumps. "Are you sure it's okay that we're here? We're kind of trespassing, aren't we?"

"Well, we would be if I didn't own it." He waved

his hand toward one of two benches on either side, then he lit a brass lantern hanging over the table and sat on the opposite bench.

Jess settled back and soaked in the ambiance of an era gone by. There was something so special about the yacht in spite of its current dilapidated state. The paint on the white-beaded panels was chipped and worn, and the mahogany woodwork had lost all traces of the gleaming varnish it must have once boasted. The tarnished brass fittings were in need of a polish. But she could almost squint her eyes and imagine how magnificent it had once been and still could be.

"So this boat is yours?"

He nodded, his eyes sparkling with pride. "It's a 1929 Herreshoff." He glanced at her. "Which means nothing to you. But trust me, it's a work of art, a sculpture that glides on the water. I inherited it from my grandfather when I was too young to appreciate what it was. It had fallen into disrepair long before it was mine and lay idle for years. A few years ago, I, um... found myself with some time on my hands, so I made it a project."

Jess took in the sight. "It must have been so beautiful in its prime."

"I'm hoping to bring it back to its former glory." He chuckled. "I've finished the work on the outside, but as you can see, I've got my work cut out for me here. But it's getting there."

Jess took in the galley and the benches that doubled as sleeping quarters. A door on the end hung open to reveal a small bathroom. "A person could live here."

"I've thought about it." He smiled. "But it would need more work on the hull before I'd feel comfortable taking it on a long trip or even leaving it here in the water year-round."

Jess's eyes widened. "We're not going to sink, are we?"

Mark's eyes sparkled with amusement. "No, we're okay. But these boats weren't really built to last a hundred years, so it's best suited to light use until I can afford to have the hull rebuilt."

"Growing up here, I guess you must know your way around a sailboat."

He laughed. "Yeah. I've done my share of sailing. I'd love to sail down the coast someday."

"That sounds exciting, and maybe a little scary."

"No, not to me. Have you sailed?"

"Never."

"There's nothing like it out there with the smell of the sea and the wind at your back." He made a good case for sailing—and him. The light in his eyes when he spoke of it made her wish she could sail with him to see what he saw and feel what he felt.

Mark leaned back and stretched his legs out. "You mentioned you haven't been lucky."

"Did I?"

His memory was a little too good. He leaned closer and tilted his head. *Is his mouth turning up at the corner?*

"Oh yeah. I guess I did." She tried to think of some way to divert the line of conversation but drew a blank. "Well, it's not much of a story." She took a breath, hesitating. *Does he need to know this?* Then she blurted out, "I was engaged. It fell apart a few months ago, and I just got laid off from my job. So, not lucky. End of story." *Excellent portrait, Jess. He can't wait to spend time with you now.*

He studied her for a moment with a look she couldn't quite read. It was soft, but it wasn't pity. She was grateful for that.

Finally, his mouth spread to a smile. "You're not much of a storyteller, are you?"

Jess leaned her head back and laughed. "No, but I'm brief. Lucky for you!" She was still smiling. Until she turned and looked into his eyes.

He smiled gently. "So, you're free of that fool of a fiancé, and your boss didn't deserve you."

She couldn't help but smile back. "I like your

version better than mine." Jess was getting better at meeting his gaze, but it still felt as though he could see more than she wanted him to—as though he understood her—and she wasn't sure she was comfortable with that.

He leaned back and stretched his arms along the tops of the benches, looking far more at ease than she felt. "So what brings you to Applecross Cove?" It was the sort of question anyone might ask out of politeness, but the way he peered at her didn't feel all that casual, at least not in her experience.

She assumed her fallback countenance of light and pleasant, which was what she wished she felt but so rarely did. "I wanted to see how far I could go without leaving the country. So here I am."

"Yes, you are."

Jess managed to avert her gaze, only to stall at his lips. She caught herself staring and averted her eyes to focus on the brass lantern that swayed as the water lapped up against the white cedar planks of the hull.

"Listen," Mark said. "It's stopped raining."

Jess came to her senses. Had he not spoken, she might have remained fully ensconced in the moment, lulled by the lapping of water and mesmerized by the intriguing Mark Breton. Which was unrealistic—if not crazy—and definitely not part of her plan.

"Oh, good," she said with an unnaturally high

pitch that was meant to sound cheery but instead sounded strained. "Well, that worked out." She stood up abruptly—"Ow!"—and bumped her head on the ceiling.

He put his hand on her head protectively, which she didn't mind at all, as she climbed out of the cabin. The afternoon air smelled of the storm and the sea, and dark storm clouds still lingered above. They walked together to the intersection of the main path and the path leading up to Mark's cottage and stood face-to-face. Perhaps it was the mild scent of wild beach roses lining the white wooden fence, but Jess felt a distinct yet inexplicable urge to lean forward and kiss him.

Mark broke the spell. "Can you find your way back? Just follow the walkway and cross the driveway. Yours is the last one." His mouth quirked at the corner. "Can't miss it."

Did he know she was close to kissing him? Or did she just look that lost? Either way, he'd spoken up just in time to stop her from embarrassing herself. So he must have known. But how could he? *Maybe he felt it too—and found it revolting.*

"So how long have you lived in this little cluster of cottages?" Jess asked. *Did that sound like a desperate attempt to stay with him?*

"Since just after high school. I needed, well

wanted, a place of my own, and Aunt Wanda let me stay here until I could afford to pay rent."

"Oh." Jess lifted her chin and thoughtfully nodded. "What about school? College?"

His mouth turned up at the corner. "I wouldn't dream of boring you with any of that."

Jess raised her eyebrows. "Oh, I'm not easily bored."

He raised an eyebrow. "Neither am I, as a rule."

What is that supposed to mean? Whatever he was thinking, the smile that came next was almost too charming for her to care.

"I'd better let you get home to dry off," he said. "We can't have you coming down with a cold."

"Actually, that's a myth. You catch a cold from a virus. Anyway, bye." Jess waved goodbye over her shoulder. *No, that wasn't at all nerdy, Jess.*

She winced and kept walking then turned and headed for her cottage, feeling more confused and attracted to Mark by the minute—and troubled by the fact that she couldn't get an accurate read on the guy. At times it seemed like he was trying to charm her. Well, the truth was, he didn't have to try very hard. He was one of those guys who was so good-looking, so masculine, and so nice that a mere passing gaze was like a tractor beam that took in all within a certain range. She'd known a few people like that.

Who was to say Mark wasn't just another guy who, with no effort, drew women to him like a human bug zapper?

She could practically hear herself sizzling.

SIX

Jess functioned best when she had a routine. It wasn't until graduate school that she'd figured that out, but better late than never. Staying focused while working from home was going to be a challenge, but she was determined.

Every morning at seven, she got up and allowed herself thirty minutes for breakfast and coffee on the deck overlooking the ocean. Then her phone alarm would go off, and she would head back inside to start working through the day with a short break for lunch. After a week, she'd discovered that she was not the only one around there who had a routine.

At 7:15, right on cue, Mark was there at the edge of his dock. Jess looked forward to it like some people looked forward to watching the news to begin their day. This brought on a pang of concern. *What if this is how deranged stalkers get started?*

With or without Mark to look at, Jess enjoyed her mornings, sipping coffee and staring out at the sea. From her vantage point, the water was soothing. But it could be as unpredictable and as volatile as life. It could buoy up massive vessels or swallow them into its depths, either on a whim or in concert with the weather. Or it could be as blue as the sky it reflected. She wondered if that was what Mark thought about as he stood there so still.

At 7:25, give or take a few minutes, Mark would head back up the dock to his cottage and close the door. And that was the last Jess would see of him until he went for his morning run. Although it was none of her business, she wondered—not just about his morning routine but about him. She felt oddly connected to him, or rather to his routine. They were like two figurines in an old Swiss clock, compelled by their mechanical fate to emerge and give the appearance of living, only to be pulled back into their separate compartments and left to their own devices. Maybe that was what attracted her to him. She recognized a kindred sense of detachment that could only come from sorrow. Another wounded soul was the last thing she needed in her life.

Jess got up and headed inside to work. She had

almost three months' severance pay until the specter of financial doom would descend on her life. Her current business covered utilities and groceries, but she needed to drum up some new online clients to fill in the gap. The end of her severance would come more quickly than she realized, so she had to be ready to take over and fend for herself when the time came. One thing she would not do was rely on credit. She would do the best with the skills she possessed while she built her business. With that in mind, she opened her laptop and began to put together some marketing materials.

Four hours later, Jess took a sip of cold coffee and grimaced. She was just getting up to head for the microwave when someone knocked. She opened the door to find Mark. He wore an old pair of jeans and one of his usual T-shirts that looked form-fitted to his muscles.

She hadn't forgotten that smile, but her heart quickened as though she were seeing it for the first time. "Hi." *Brilliant beginning, Jess. And remember, an hour ago, when you were going to put some deodorant on but got sidetracked?*

He glanced past her to the computer. "I'm sorry. Am I interrupting?"

"No, not at all." She took a step back. "Come on in."

"Are you sure? You seemed a little... dismayed."

Well, that's just great. He can read minds. Jess peered into his eyes and tried to decide whether honesty was, in fact, the best policy. *Oh, why not?* "No, you're fine." She frowned. "I just realized that I got up and started working, and I haven't really brushed my hair or—"

"Dressed?"

Her eyes widened, and she glanced down at her oversized sleep T-shirt. "Oh. That too." All she could do was offer a helpless shrug.

Mark laughed, which eased some of her tension, if not her embarrassment. "I just had a craving for seafood, and I thought, well, I wondered if you might want to join me for lunch."

Jess's eyes lit up. "Oh, that sounds good!" She glanced away for a moment as a sudden realization struck her. "I just remembered. I haven't eaten yet."

"You forgot to eat? What's that like?" He appeared way too amused.

"It's like this but dressed better."

"There's no dress code where we're going. You just need to look as good as a lobsterman fresh off the boat." He leaned toward her slightly. "So the bar's pretty low."

Jess started to mentally go down her list of goals for the day to make sure she could spare the time, then she gave up, pleased for the diversion. "Okay. Give me a minute?"

"Sure."

"Have a seat. Make yourself at home." Without waiting to see his reaction, she rushed into her room and closed the door. After a couple of deep, cleansing breaths, she burst into a flurry of activity. *It's just lunch. Not a date.* She caught sight of herself in the mirror then closed her eyes tightly and turned away. *Just put on a T-shirt and jeans and be done with it.*

No more than five minutes later, Jess inspected herself in the mirror, impressed at how quickly she could get it together. *Not bad. Not good, but... Hair brushed—check. Teeth—ack!* She emerged from her room, held up a finger, and hastily uttered, "Just a second." Then she disappeared into the bathroom. *Teeth brushed—done.* She peered at the mirror, gave her hair a quick fluff, then exhaled. *Best I can do on short notice.*

MARK WAS SPRAWLED on the sofa, looking completely at home, when Jess emerged from her bathroom.

"Look at you, wearing clothes! Very nice!" He gave an approving nod and stood. "Ready?" While Jess locked the door, Mark said, "I thought you might be going stir crazy after a week alone."

That sounded a lot like a disclaimer, or worse—pity. "Yeah? I guess. Honestly, I'm pretty comfortable with my own company. I've done a little solo traveling, so it actually doesn't bother me, being alone."

"Oh, good." He walked quietly on.

Jess wondered if she'd overplayed her hand on that one. He was only being neighborly, and she'd practically shot him down for the gesture. Her next words came out a little too cheery. "But it's good to have company." He nodded and smiled politely in her direction. Why did she feel so nervous? It wasn't like this was a date. He probably would have done the same for anyone new to town who was renting his aunt's cottage.

He was avoiding eye contact, which wasn't a good sign. She tried again to break down the wall she'd put up between them. "I could use some advice on where the good seafood places are."

He reacted pleasantly enough, but a glint of what looked like amusement brightened his eyes. "They're literally lining the harbor."

She winced. "That makes sense, what with the ocean being right there." This was not going well, but Jess blamed herself. She'd set the tone. Now she was making it even more awkward.

An hour later, they sat at a table in Cal's Place, a rustic seafood shack that looked out at the cove. Jess had settled into a more comfortable frame of mind, brought on by her mouth being too full to embarrass herself. But then the meal ended, and their plates were cleared. Any sensible, neighborly guy would have put them both out of their misery and suggested they leave, but for some reason, Mark chose to prolong the social agony with coffee.

Jess gazed out at the harbor. At some point during the meal, clouds had tumbled in over the ocean. "Looks like we've lost the sun." Everything that came out of her mouth was so abjectly uninteresting. She wanted to get up, thank him for lunch, and make a hasty exit. She tried to tell herself doing so would be performing a service for Mark, but she couldn't think of a way to execute it without seeming rude.

She'd had months to get over Adam, so that couldn't be the problem. Maybe she was just out of practice. It had been so long since she'd spent time with a man—especially an attractive one—that she'd come completely unhinged. She could only attribute Mark's continued presence to unwavering manners.

He took a sip of coffee and stared out the window. An afternoon fog was rolling in. "I love days like this. It's good weather for reading."

"You like to read?"

His eyebrows drew together. "I think I just said that I did."

Jess didn't know what to say. She reminded herself that she was a perfectly intelligent woman, capable of conversing. *So what is my problem?*

A crooked grin formed on his lips.

Jess exhaled. "I'm sorry."

He seemed genuinely surprised. "Why?"

"I... I don't know. I think you were right. A week alone has rendered me socially inept. Poor you."

A gentle smile warmed the light in his eyes. "It's okay."

Jess's eyes narrowed to an incredulous squint, but he had a stillness about him that was convincing.

"I went through a phase where I spent a little too much time alone," Mark said. "I recognize some of the signs."

"Signs?"

"I don't want to intrude on your personal space. I just thought you could use a friend here in town."

Jess wasn't sure whether to thank or reject him. He made it too easy for her to let her guard down, and she wasn't ready for that. She barely knew him, so she needed to be cautious. People could only hurt her if she let them. She'd learned that the hard way.

"If I'm way off base..." He shook his head with a self-deprecating smirk. "Sorry. Forget I said anything."

His eyes flickered toward the door, and he leaned back as though he were getting ready to leave.

"No, you're right." Their eyes met, and she took a chance. "I could use a friend."

A kind warmth lit his eyes. "I can be that."

Tension she didn't know she'd been carrying lifted. *A friend.* That was probably better for her than the attraction she'd been harboring since she'd met him.

She smiled. It was official. She had a new home and a friend.

JESS WENT HOME and stared at her to-do list. Before she got halfway through it, she gazed distractedly out the window.

Friendship is better than romance.

The thing was, it was true—at least it was for her at this point in her life. Moving there had been part of her plan to regain order and control. There was room in that plan for a friend. Romance was better left on hold. She had come too far to let a romantic entanglement ruin her progress.

So she reviewed the next steps of her plan: set aside thoughts of men, build the business, save money, and find peace and strength. Alone.

SEVEN

THE FOLLOWING FRIDAY, Jess was feeling good about all she'd accomplished during the week—so good, in fact, that she decided to indulge in a second cup of morning coffee outside on her deck. It was a glorious day. A couple of sailboats were heading out of the harbor and hoisting their white sails against a clear blue sky. If she couldn't feel content looking at that, there was no hope for her.

She smiled and looked at her wrist then remembered her watch was in its charger. Either she'd come out too early, or Mark was running late as he made his way down to the dock for that water-staring thing that he did. But that morning was different. When he arrived at his usual place, instead of standing and staring out at the sea, he pulled off his shirt and stood poised at the edge of the dock in what she realized weren't shorts but swim trunks.

That sight was enough to warrant lingering on the deck for a third cup of coffee. The coffee was optional. Seeing him shirtless was not.

He dove into the water, swam out to a buoy, then swam back and pulled himself onto the dock. Having given up all shame by that point, Jess entertained the idea of buying a pair of binoculars.

Mark wrapped a towel around his shoulders, prompting Jess to wonder how cold the water was. He sat on a bench then bent down and buried his face in his hands. He was turned so she couldn't see his face, but it almost seemed like he was crying.

Suddenly feeling as if she were intruding, Jess slid down in her chair. She reminded herself that she barely knew him. He might've just been cold or thinking really hard, like the Rodin sculpture but with two hands. Yet she'd watched him each morning since she'd arrived, and that day, something was different.

No. Something was wrong.

His posture was slumped over, defeated. She wanted to go to him to see if she could help. A friend would do something like that, and she was his friend. But there were friends, and then there were *friends*. On the friendship continuum, theirs fell more toward the acquaintance side. If she went to him at that moment, she would only be intruding, so she resisted the urge and instead simply sat there and watched.

Finally, Jess heaved a sigh. *This is ridiculous.* She was inventing all sorts of drama that just wasn't there. *Probably.*

With no warning, Mark reached up, smoothed his hair back, and wiped his face with his hands. Then he got up and walked back to his cottage. He turned to look in her direction, but she slid farther down in her chair and hid behind the tall shrubs that lined her deck. Through a gap in the leaves, she watched him until he was inside his cottage, then she went back inside to work.

He was on her mind on and off throughout the rest of the morning. He wasn't exactly the emotional type— at least not that she'd seen. Mark was one of those nice, laid-back guys, a bit lacking in the ambition department, but agreeably so. He obviously liked his hometown and the life he'd known growing up. He'd never mentioned college, which was fine.

Having obtained a master's degree, Jess was inclined to find education a bit overrated. She couldn't think of any knowledge she'd acquired in a bachelor's or master's program that she couldn't have gotten from reading a book—well, lots of books. Of course, she had to concede that feedback from professors and classroom discussions could yield results that could not be found in books, but work and life were good teachers as well.

So who was she to judge Mark for not being a hard-driving type A with different ambitions and priorities? He'd taken a path in life that made him happy. How many people could say that?

Even so, what she'd seen earlier made her wonder. If Mark was so laid-back and easygoing, what had that been all about? She couldn't be sure. She'd been too far away. Body language wasn't exactly a science. Maybe he'd been slumped over because his back had hurt from swimming for the first time in... whenever. *What do I know?* Nothing, except she must have had too much time on her hands and too little ambition of her own to get her business off the ground. Otherwise, she wouldn't have been making up stories about good-looking neighbors who had their own lives and didn't need her help.

So it was official. Being alone was messing with her head. She thought for a moment then picked up her phone and typed out a text to her best friend, Maddie.

Everything's going great. And good news: I've been talking to myself so much, I've become kind of fascinating!

She'd been lost in a web-design project for most of the morning when her phone rang. Her best friend's photo filled the screen.

Jess quickly tapped her phone to answer. "Maddie?"

"Hi, Jess! What are you doing?"

Jess set her phone to speaker, set it down on the table, and studied the screen as she scrolled down its contents. "Right now? Working."

"Yeah, me too. So, this is a little last minute, but I was wondering if you had plans for the weekend."

Jess brightened. "Wanna come for a visit?"

"Oh! Well, if you insist."

Jess leaned back in her chair and smiled. "I do."

"Yay! I'll take tomorrow afternoon off and drive over. Gotta go. See you later. Bye!"

"Bye."

Jess stared at her phone. "I must have scared Maddie with that text about talking to myself." She chuckled then suddenly stopped. "But I *am* talking to myself!"

Maddie knocked on the door the next afternoon at four. Jess greeted her friend with a hug and whisked her inside for the ten-second grand tour of the cottage.

"It's so adorable!" Maddie combed her fingers through her cropped auburn hair and pushed her sunglasses up to the top of her head. She then reached into a reusable shopping bag and pulled out a bottle of wine. "Enough with the formalities. Let's open this bad boy and get down to business." She leveled a look at Jess. "I want to know everything."

Jess took the wine and headed into the kitchen for a corkscrew. "First things first." Minutes later, they were comfortably seated cross-legged on the sofa with wine, popcorn, and chocolates all within reach.

"So about this guy Mark." Jess made a face, but Maddie held up her palm. "Don't even try to deny it."

"Deny what?" Jess had always thought she had a pretty good poker face, but Maddie's expression disabused her of that apparent delusion. "What gave me away?"

Maddie wasn't even trying to suppress her triumphant expression. "I think it was the way you typed 'Mark' in your texts."

"Texts? I may have casually mentioned him in passing. Once."

"Yeah, that was the one. 'My friend Mark.'" She practically sang the last word. "Or was it 'My friend, *smiley face with hearts, face with heart eyes, big heart,* Mark, *fire.*'"

"I did not do that!"

Maddie leaned closer. "The emojis were implied."

Jess rolled her eyes. "Oh, right."

"Well, he's got at least one thing going for him."

Jess stared at her friend, refusing to play.

Maddie waited then heaved a sigh and gave up. "He's not Adam."

Jess glanced at her watch. "Hmm. Twenty-three minutes before mentioning Adam."

Maddie lifted her eyebrows and averted her eyes.

Jess wasn't surprised. Maddie had given up long ago on trying to pretend she liked Adam. Given how things had turned out with him, Jess couldn't blame her. The truth was, Jess still kicked herself for not having seen all his character faults on her own. "You're right. He's not Adam, and he's not my... anything."

Maddie was suddenly serious. "Well, I wish he could be. You deserve to be happy." Genuine regret shone in her eyes.

Jess leaned back, resigned. "So do a lot of people. But we have to live with our choices, and Adam wasn't my best. You tried to tell me. The stupidest thing is, I think I knew from the start that we were way too different. But being with him was like playing dress-up."

Maddie's face brightened. "I'll say one thing for him. He had really nice suits."

Jess nodded. "He did. And he looked great in

them. But that's the thing. He was all about fine things and nice restaurants. We went through all the motions, but for him, it was never really about me. I was just one of the things he liked having around."

Maddie exhaled slowly but refrained from saying out loud what they'd rehashed so many times. Jess had been blind to Adam's flaws for too long, but in the end, they had been impossible to ignore.

Silence settled for a moment, then Jess said, "You know, there were times when all I really wanted was some simple sign that he cared. Something thoughtful, you know—like a book he'd seen that he thought I might like, or I don't know, something small that made him think of me. But that was the problem. He didn't think of me."

Maddie sat taller. "Well, that's all over, and life will go on. It has gone on! Look at you here with your adorable cottage and your smokin'-hot neighbor."

Jess protested. "I never said smokin' hot... or even hot." She shrugged nonchalantly. "He might be considered attractive."

A knock on the door interrupted them.

Maddie raised her eyebrows. "Expecting company?"

Jess shook her head and went to answer the door. When she opened it, the man before her took her breath away. "Mark!"

"I got some pizza, and I—" He stopped speaking when he spotted Maddie. "I'm sorry. I didn't know you had company."

"I'm not company. I'm Maddie." She got up and went to the door to shake his hand. "Here, I'll take that. Come on in." Pizza in hand, Maddie pivoted around so only Jess would see her mouth the word *"Hot!"*

Jess stepped back and gestured for him to come in, but he winced. "I don't want to intrude."

Maddie called out from the kitchen, "Don't worry, you're not!" When she returned with plates and napkins, she was rewarded with a sharp look from Jess. But as they distributed pizza, everything seemed to settle down... until Maddie's mouth stopped being full of pizza. "So, Mark, are you from around here?"

"Yes."

"What do you do?"

He shrugged amiably. "I wear a few hats."

"One at a time, or do you just stack them up?"

"Excuse me, Mark," Jess cut in. "Maddie's practicing to become a police interrogator."

Mark cast warm eyes on Jess and turned to Maddie. "One at a time. Baseball cap for landscaping, same thing but backwards for home-maintenance jobs, an occasional hard hat for construction projects, and no hat for real estate."

Maddie beamed. "And where did you go to school?"

"Here."

A look of confusion came and went as Maddie observed Mark's eyes flicker toward Jess then settle downward.

"Oh, got it," Maddie said. "High school. So no college?"

Jess's jaw dropped. She stood up. "Water anyone?"

Mark looked up and smiled, but it was forced. "No, thanks. I just remembered I left some beer in the car. Be right back."

As soon as the door closed behind him, Maddie asked, "What did I do?"

Jess took a moment to collect herself. "Well, you might want to ease up on the questions."

"I'm helping you, Jess—asking questions you want to but won't."

"I've barely spent any time with the guy, but you're grilling him like you're my dad and he's just asked for permission to court me."

"I like your dad."

"So do I. And I like Mark too. Let's not scare him away."

Maddie appeared so dismayed that Jess reassured her. "It's okay. I'm sure he knows you didn't mean anything by it."

Maddie's eyebrows drew together, but before she could speak, Mark knocked and walked inside looking triumphant. "Can't believe I forgot this." He held out the six-pack of craft beer to Maddie and Jess, but they declined with a wave. He walked into the kitchen and put his beer in the fridge, keeping one for himself.

He sat down and looked directly at Maddie. "I was in a car accident on senior prom night, and I put off going to college."

"I'm sorry," Jess said softly.

He wrinkled his face as though it were nothing, but Jess sensed that wasn't the case.

Maddie brightened. "But you recovered."

He nodded. "We all did."

"You were lucky," Maddie said.

Mark's eyes were somber and dark. "Yeah. It could have been worse."

"More pizza, anyone?" Maddie held out the box toward Mark and then Jess.

Jess was desperate to change the subject. "Board games? Never mind. I'm not sure where they are. I've got a few boxes I haven't unpacked."

"Movie!" Maddie reached for the remote. Minutes later, they were lined up on the sofa with their feet propped up on the coffee table, passing popcorn and watching an action movie.

Jess sat in the middle and tried to ignore how her

heart skipped a beat when Mark's shoulder touched hers.

MADDIE SPOKE through her smile and waved as Mark pulled out of the driveway. "So he's gorgeous."

Jess closed the door and busied herself with clearing plates and glasses.

Maddie reached out. "Not that one!"

Jess handed the wine glass to her and went back to clearing.

Maddie pointed. "Or that one."

Jess paused. "That's mine."

"I know." Maddie poured the rest of the bottle into their glasses then plopped down on an overstuffed chair. "So tell me..."

Jess leveled a look and sat down on the sofa. "Not gonna happen. I'm here to put my life back in order and to start up a business."

Maddie leaned forward, looking helpless. "I know, but he's so..."

Jess was already nodding. "I know."

Maddie sighed. "Blue eyes, athletic body." She lifted her chin and stared off into the distance. "Let's just take a moment to reflect on that."

"If you weren't holding a glass of red wine, I'd have already thrown this pillow at you."

"Fine. You can reflect on your independent life. I have no such restrictions."

Jess rolled her eyes. "Okay, yes. He is hot. It's pretty hard to ignore. And believe me, I've tried. I've only recently managed to hide his effect on me."

"Blushing? Misty-eyed gazing? Nope. You're not hiding a thing."

Jess sighed, defeated.

Maddie peered closely at her. "He likes you."

"Maybe. And I like him too. But I think you're forgetting what I've been through."

Maddie looked at Jess as though she'd lost her mind. "Oh, I seriously doubt that. I feel like I lived it with you. I basically did. But Adam was an aberration. That's not going to happen again. Guys don't typically day trade away the dream house down payment. At least that's a first from what I've seen."

"Ten years of savings." Jess took a sip of her wine, then the tears welled up in her eyes. "It was our dream home. To start our dream life."

Maddie winced and shook her head. "I didn't see it coming. He seemed so perfect. A stockbroker. Have I mentioned those suits?"

"Yeah. Then he quit his job so he could make his fortune day trading. I had no idea he was addicted and beginning a downward descent. So you'll forgive me for being reluctant to trust someone I've only just met." She drew in a deep breath and exhaled. She fixed her eyes on Maddie. "I feel good. My life feels secure. My days are peaceful and predictable."

"I know, but—"

"It's not a good time to jump out of the mess I was in only to land in the great unknown."

Maddie took a big swig of wine. "If by 'great unknown' you mean those muscular arms, I would risk it."

Jess couldn't help but laugh. "That's the wine talking. In the clear light of day, those broad shoulders and arms won't look nearly as hot."

Maddie lifted an eyebrow.

Jess slumped her shoulders.

Then they both said in unison, "Yeah, they will."

EIGHT

THEIR GIRLS' weekend passed quickly. They explored hiking trails, local shops, and seaside restaurants in equal measure. Jess hadn't realized how much she'd missed laughter, but Maddie did her best to bring Jess back up to speed. By the time Maddie pulled out of the driveway, Jess was happy, exhausted, and most of all, hopeful. Maddie did that for her. She had a way of listening and caring then making Jess laugh her way out of her troubles.

When Jess had gone through the worst of her big engagement fail, Maddie had been there through it all, at times dragging Jess through the dark tunnel she'd been lost in. But they'd gotten through it together. And when Jess lost her job, Maddie had brought over a shopping bag full of comfort food. They'd watched rom-coms and forgotten for a couple of hours that life could be hard. No matter what life threw at her, Maddie could always make Jess laugh. That was her greatest gift next to friendship.

Jess smiled and walked into the cottage, feeling good about life. Everything was on track with her new home and new business. The money was going to take time, but she had enough to get by. If she didn't feel entirely happy, she could see it on the distant horizon. There was no timetable for happiness, but she had work to do now. So she would stay busy until she achieved it.

MONDAY CAME and went with no sign of Mark. She tried not to think about how thoughts of him had invaded her days. So what if she had a little crush? It was harmless and maybe even therapeutic. Anything that kept her mind off Adam was a good thing. Although, as infatuations went, this was a little extreme for her. Her usual method of dealing with life's challenges was to dig into work and bury her personal feelings. She was still forging ahead with her business plan, but somewhere along the line, she'd made space in her thoughts for Mark. Maddie had not helped in that regard. With the subtlety of a used car salesman, she'd encouraged Jess to view Mark as a romantic prospect. Maddie would be proud if she knew how successful she'd been.

While visions of possibilities floated through Jess's thoughts, she managed to make some ad graphics and placed social media ads that brought in a trickle of new clients. So she had no shortage of ways to keep busy and take her mind off Mark.

On Tuesday morning, Jess came up for air after an especially busy morning. She was just about to take a break when she heard something outside. She peeked through the blinds and found Wanda on her knees in the flower bed under her window. She went outside.

Wanda gazed up jovially from under a wide-brimmed straw hat. "Hello!"

"Hi!" Jess smiled and came closer.

"I've been meaning to stop by to see how you were settling in."

"I'm all settled, and I love it!"

Wanda's eyes gleamed with delight. "Good. Oh! I've brought you a housewarming gift."

Jess wasn't expecting a gift from her landlady. That was a first.

Wanda lifted a basket of flowers cut from the garden. "This is part of it. Hold on." She disappeared around the corner. A car door slammed, and she returned with a vase. She put a handful of flowers in the vase and held it out to Jess. "You'll need to add water."

"How pretty!"

"Those are two of my hobbies—gardening and pottery."

Jess looked with incredulity at the beautiful vase. "You made this?"

"I did."

"Well, it's gorgeous! I love the colors!"

A familiar male voice interrupted them. "Hello?" Mark rounded the corner. He glanced at Jess then focused on Wanda. "I saw your car." Mark gave his aunt Wanda a hug then turned to Jess with enough momentum that she thought he might hug her too. *Wishful thinking on my part.* "Hi, Jess."

"Mark." *Am I smiling too much?* "Out enjoying the weather?" *Am I talking about weather too much?* She averted her eyes. She was definitely thinking too much about what she was saying. She reminded herself it was small talk, not iambic pentameter. Her mind wandered back to the weather and how it felt ten degrees warmer all of a sudden. Her eyes flicked back to Mark as she made an effort to pull it together. Her mouth felt suddenly dry. "Would anyone like something to drink? Lemonade? Water?"

Mark smiled with a warmth that made his eyes

sparkle and her knees weaken. "Lemonade sounds good."

"Water for me." Wanda's eyes had their own twinkle as she looked from Jess to her nephew.

"Why don't we go inside?" Jess asked.

Wanda gazed helplessly down at herself. "I've been kneeling in dirt. But why don't you go in, Mark, and help?"

His eyebrows drew together for an instant, then he recovered and held out his arm, inviting Jess to go first. Just before she walked past him, Jess caught Mark raising an eyebrow at his aunt.

Inside, Jess busied herself getting glasses and drinks. She felt awkward and nervous.

"So Maddie's gone home?"

"Yes. It was a quick weekend visit."

"You two seem pretty close."

"We are." Jess handed Mark a glass of lemonade. "We've been friends since college. She's one of those people you don't come across often. Someone you could turn to no matter what. She's a really good friend."

Mark held the door, and the two walked outside.

"I'm back here!" Wanda called out from the deck. "I'm enjoying the shade and the breeze."

The three of them chatted. When they'd finished

their drinks, Wanda said, "I've got to go back to the office, but you two stay and enjoy the sea breeze." She turned to Jess. "Don't get up. It was so nice to see you. Have a great afternoon." Then, with a wave, she was off.

Jess and Mark listened as Wanda's car started then crunched over the gravel driveway and onto the road.

Mark gave Jess a bashful grin. "Subtle, isn't she?"

That took Jess by surprise. Of course he would have noticed Wanda's behavior too. But with that out in the open, Jess wasn't sure what to say. That put things on a new level. To acknowledge Wanda's matchmaking efforts was to acknowledge that she and Mark could be together. After all of Jess's work convincing herself it was only a harmless crush, Wanda had just made it real. Not that real was a bad thing. It was just that it made it a thing. Emotions could now be invested. And she'd learned the hard way that investments didn't always work out.

"Aunt Wanda likes you," Mark said.

Jess tried to look casually pleased, but her heart was flip-flopping. "I like her too."

He gazed into her eyes. "I like you too."

She felt a little breathless. She took a quiet, calming breath. He had said it before. He just meant as a friend. "I..." She suddenly wanted to pour out all her feelings—what she'd gone through with Adam and why she was desperately, shockingly, pathetically attracted to Mark—but the timing was off, so it just couldn't be.

Mark seemed so calm. She didn't know how he did that. "I like being around you." He leaned back. "Don't worry. It doesn't have to be any more than that." He met her gaze directly. No one had ever looked at her like that—like what she said really mattered.

"I wasn't worried. I..." Her head was swimming. "I like you too." Jess was overwhelmed with conflicting emotions. *What am I doing? I'm not ready for this.* Adam had left her in pieces that she hadn't quite put back together. She had cocooned herself into her cozy cottage, and for the first time in so long, she felt emotionally safe. Until that moment. With four little words, Mark had pierced the protective shell of her heart, exposing a surprising amount of unsettled emotion.

He smiled softly. "But?" This tall, sturdy, muscular man looked so gently at her, Jess feared a tear might betray what a mess she was inside. But his manner had a calming effect. Not that it entirely cured her nervousness, but it took the edge off.

She gazed into his eyes. "I want it to be about six months from now when my life is more settled."

A spark lit his eyes. "It will be. We don't have to rush it."

Their eyes met, and Jess felt a weight lift that she

hadn't even known was there. She knew she had baggage, but she hadn't realized she was dragging around a full set of hard-sided luggage with the expandable zippers. With absolute certainty, she knew they'd arrived at an unvoiced understanding. They could be friends. It could grow into more, or not. They could take time to figure it out.

Mark set down his glass and stood up. "I'd better let you get back to work."

Jess stood up to join him.

"Thanks for the lemonade." He gazed at her for a moment, touched the deck post, and walked away.

NINE

Jess and Mark were friends. There was no pressure for more, which of course meant Mark was all Jess could think of. He had given her space—unexpected, unselfish, and cavernous space for her wild, uncooperative heart to treat like a vacuum that she could fill with what-ifs. Which was why, three days later, she felt lost.

What scared her the most wasn't Mark or his feelings but hers. From the moment she'd met him, she had felt a deep, undeniable attraction that threatened to be her undoing. To her credit, she knew herself well. She didn't fall often, but when she did, it was fast and deep. And once she was drowning in her own emotions, there was no turning back. So she'd learned to be cautious, which she needed to be, especially now. She could not let herself tumble over the edge for another man who could prove as disappointing as Adam. Falling in love with dashing good looks and a well-tailored suit was no substitute for the real thing—true love. And that was what she was desperately holding out for. Until then, she wanted to feel more sure-footed before anything headed that way.

Mark, of course, was the opposite of Adam. He was laid-back. His life was slow-paced, and he took time to live it and enjoy his surroundings. And he listened. He gave Jess more attention than she'd ever received, and that was addictive. Looking into someone's eyes, undistracted, was such a simple thing. At first, she'd told herself he was being polite. But now she was sure there was more. He had made that much clear. That was one more thing she liked about him—he was plain and direct. She liked—no, she loved that. But she had rewarded him for it by pushing him away.

She stared out the window, daydreaming about what he might be doing, and she wished she were there with him, doing whatever he was.

Good work, Jess. Now you've done it. You've driven away the one man who might be right for you—out of fear that he won't.

She heaved a great sigh and decided that this and the other pressing world problems would be best managed with a fresh cup of coffee. She stopped halfway to the kitchen, deciding to treat herself to a takeout coffee and a midafternoon walk on the pier. Maybe she would go nuts and treat herself to one of those huge evil muffins from The Bean Counter, a coffee shop owned by an ex-accountant friend of Wanda's.

It was one of those gray days on which the mist brushed her face as she strolled the short distance to town. The air and the water were practically still except for the rhythmic clang of a bell buoy in the harbor. A few preseason tourists meandered about. All in all, it was just as Jess had hoped it would be, the sort of morning for losing herself in her thoughts while she savored a fresh cup of hot coffee. And... yes, why not? A muffin the size of a layer cake.

Once she had her coffee and muffin in hand, she walked past the dockside bar Mark had taken her to, which would have redirected her thoughts to him if they hadn't already been there. Now all she needed was a bench where she could sit and savor her midmorning treats.

Mark sat at his favorite table in Cal's Place, looking out at the pier, lost in thought about his favorite subject of late—his new neighbor, Jess.

Two coffees appeared on the table, and Mark

glanced up to see his high school friend Cal Jr., who ran the place for his semiretired father, Cal Sr.

"Thanks, Cal." Mark smiled and nodded as Cal took the seat next to his.

They talked about business, the weather, and their favorite teams. Then Mark spotted Jess outside, walking along the pier toward the end. He caught himself staring a little too long to be taking in the overall view. He felt Cal's eyes on him and glanced over. Cal had that knowing look on his face that was so damned annoying at times, but Mark acted as though nothing had happened.

Cal's mouth quirked at the corner. "Okay. Don't tell me."

"Don't tell you what?"

Cal rolled his eyes. "Oh, I don't know. Why you're staring at your new neighbor, for starters."

Mark made a feeble attempt at a laugh. "You're imagining things."

"Like that basset hound look on your face?"

Mark smirked then sat straighter and lifted his chin.

"C'mon, Mark, you owe me the truth—if for no other reason than for my not parking myself at your table with my chin in my hands when you brought her in here before."

Mark said dryly, "Thanks for not embarrassing yourself. Or me."

"I didn't have to. You're doing a good job on your own." Alarm flashed through Mark's mind, but before he could respond, Cal added, "Relax. No one else knows the difference, but you and I go way back. I haven't seen you like this since the fifth grade. What was her name?"

Mark heaved a sigh. There was no escaping Cal. He was like a dog with a bone. "Lizzie Luckenbill."

Cal could barely hold in his delight as he practically sang, "Lizzie Luckenbill, with her blond ponytail that bounced up and down when she talked. What ever happened to her?"

"Assistant district attorney in Bangor."

"That's right." Cal gazed off in the distance. "Remember the time mean old Mrs. Flannery forgot to assign weekend homework? And Lizzie raised her hand and reminded her?"

Mark laughed and nodded. "Yeah. She was kind of conscientious."

"That's one word for it." Cal exhaled. "I wonder if she still has that ponytail."

Mark ignored him and stared out at the pier.

Cal would not let it go. "And now, poor Lizzie, cast aside for... What's her name?"

Mark gave Cal a deadpan look. "Jess."

"Jess?"

"Pelletier."

Cal lifted his chin. "Jess Pelletier," he mused. "And don't think I didn't see you two the other day making googly eyes at each other at this very table. What was that all about?"

Mark had to laugh. "Lunch." He couldn't help himself. He scanned the pier again, but he'd lost track of Jess.

"Bro, look at yourself." As Cal chuckled, he followed Mark's gaze outside, where a boy no older than ten sailed down the pier on a skateboard, weaving in and out of pedestrians. "Were we ever that reckless?"

Mark cast a sideways look at Cal. "I'd like to think we were smarter, but to look at you now—" He stopped midsentence and cursed as the boy lost control and ran into someone at the end of the pier. "That's Jess!" He was halfway to the door in a flash. "She can't swim," he yelled in a panic.

Cal followed Mark down the pier. By the time they arrived, someone had thrown in a life preserver from a nearby boat, but Jess couldn't reach it. Unable to swim, she was frantically flailing her arms and gasping for air.

Mark dove in, wrapped his arm across Jess's chest, and pulled her back to the pier, where he hoisted her to Cal, who lifted her out of the water. They carried her to a bench and set her down so she could cough and catch her breath.

Mark smoothed Jess's wet hair over her shoulder and rested his palm on her back. "Are you okay?"

She nodded. "I think so." She sat for a moment while her breathing grew steady. "I was just standing there, looking out at the boats. Something hit me."

A spark of anger flashed through Mark. "A kid on a skateboard."

Jess started to shiver. "Is he okay?"

"Oh, he's fine," Cal said, clearly annoyed.

Despite being soaked through himself, Mark tried to warm Jess by rubbing his hands on her shoulders and arms. "Are you up to walking?"

"Yeah, I'm fine." She stood up and faltered.

Mark circled her waist with his arm and supported her as they walked back down the pier. He looked past Jess to Cal. "Have you got something hot to drink?"

"How 'bout an Irish coffee?"

With a nod, Mark said, "I'll have one too. Hold the coffee."

Minutes later, Mark and Jess sat on the same side of a booth in Cal's bar. Mark continued to rub Jess's arms while Cal shouted orders for their drinks. "I've got a blanket in my car," he said to Mark. "I'll be right back."

"I can't stop shivering," Jess said.

Mark pulled her closer and continued to rub her arms. "The spring air might feel warmer, but the ocean temperature is probably somewhere near fifty degrees."

Cal returned with a blanket, which Mark quickly wrapped around Jess's shoulders. He took what was left for himself. "Better?"

Jess nodded, and Mark wrapped his arms back around her.

By the time Jess finished her Irish coffee, she'd stopped shivering.

Cal came over and sat on the opposite bench. "How're you doing?"

Jess managed a smile, which drew relief from Mark. He turned to Cal. "Can I borrow your car?"

"Sure." He dug into his pocket, pulled out the keys, and put them on the table. "Leave the keys in the cup holder. I'll walk over later to get it."

Mark kept Jess close as they walked to the car. He drove her back home and walked her to the door.

Jess paused and turned to Mark. "Thank you."

He shook his head. "I'm just glad I was there."

She narrowed her eyes. "Why were you there?"

"I was at Cal's, having lunch. We were at my favorite table by the window. Thank God."

She gazed into his eyes. "Thank you."

It was all he could do not to pull her into his arms

and kiss her. Instead, he shrugged. "Someone there would have done it if I hadn't been there."

"But you did it. You saved my life."

He wasn't sure how much longer he could maintain their "just friends" agreement if she kept looking at him like that. "I'm just glad you're okay. You are okay, aren't you? I could stay for a while."

"Thanks, but I'll be okay." She moved toward him slightly, or maybe he was wishing she would. He could have sworn there was a sort of magnetic pull between them. He rested his hands on her shoulders and gave them a squeeze. "Call me if you need anything. I mean it. I don't care what time it is. Okay?"

She gave a warm nod. "Thank you again."

He narrowed his eyes. "That's enough of that. Now go get some rest, and stay warm."

Her eyes shone as she smiled. Then she slipped inside the cottage.

Mark felt a sudden chill and hopped into Cal's car and drove home dreaming of a hot shower to warm him up after his impromptu dip in the harbor.

TEN

JESS WOKE WITH A GROAN. Her head ached, and her body felt sluggish. But a look in the mirror sealed the deal. Her little swim in the cold waters of the Atlantic had taken its toll. In college, she'd had adrenaline hangovers at the end of every semester. After pushing hard, losing sleep, and completing her papers and exams, she would crash. But this was a whole new energy low. She decided to give herself the day off to wallow under the covers and hoped the novel on her nightstand might help her recover.

She kept replaying the fall in her mind. The shock and confusion of finding herself in the water was distressing enough. But when she'd found herself unable to breathe, she had panicked. She'd gasped for air and frantically flailed her arms, trying to somehow pull herself out of the water. But her efforts had been useless. She'd bobbed in and out of the water then felt herself sinking. But a strong arm had clamped around her and pulled her back to the surface. She'd come so close to death, yet there she was, almost as if nothing had happened.

Jess had gone through her whole life never realizing how close death was at any given moment. That realization shook her. If she were honest with herself, she still felt its nearness. She had been in a nightmare that seemed like it couldn't have happened. But she knew it had because one thing was vividly etched in her soul—the terror. She would never forget it.

Her coffee was just about ready when a knock sounded on the front door and interrupted her plan for a hasty return to the warmth of her bed. For a brief moment, she entertained the idea of ignoring whoever it was, but she sighed and went to the door. When she opened it, surprise washed over her.

"Mark." For some reason, he was the last person she'd expected to see at her door that day, at the crack of dawn, no less. Surely he couldn't have been feeling much better than she did.

"Hi. I hope it's not too early. I was passing by, and I wanted to make sure you were okay."

"Uh, come in." She slowly blinked and tried to

clear her head. "Sorry. I'm still waking up. I didn't sleep too well."

"Me neither."

She studied him. He had color in his face, bright eyes, and was fully dressed in his usual jeans and T-shirt topped with an unzipped hoodie. Why didn't he look like crap? She knew she did.

If his always-appealing blue eyes and strong presence hadn't charmed her, what he said next did. "Why don't you sit down, and I'll bring you some coffee?"

"You save lives and get coffee? You're nice to have around." She sat and pulled a throw blanket around her shoulders. "But this is my place. Shouldn't I be serving you?"

He looked back at her on his way to the kitchen and smiled. "Not today, not after that surprise swim you took yesterday."

She grimaced playfully. "You did too."

"I prefer warmer water," he said from the kitchen. "But I used to swim twice a week in the ocean all through high school."

"Because...?"

"Because I was insane. Although I did wear a wet suit when the water was cold. Cream or sugar?"

"No, thanks. Black."

He came through the doorway with two steaming mugs of coffee.

Jess wrapped both hands around her mug. "Thanks. This is perfect. I could pretty much live on this and the muffins from The Bean Counter. Who knew accountants could cook?"

He started to sit then sprang up. "Oh! I almost forgot." He went to the hall table near the front door and retrieved a clay pot he must have set down on the way in. He handed it to her. "I guess you could call it a baptism gift." He shrugged and sat down.

"Thank you." She stared at it, puzzled. "For the dirt."

"It's a sunflower seed."

Jess was grateful for the really nice gesture, but she was dismayed by the poor sunflower's fate. She was sure she had told Mark about her lack of a green thumb, but why would he remember? She decided to get it out in the open so it wouldn't be a crushing blow when his gift met its inevitable demise. "Mark, I can't do plants. This will die."

He balked and waved her off as if that couldn't possibly happen. But he didn't know her history.

Jess cringed. "Well, I'll try not to kill it, but don't say I didn't warn you. I have priors for involuntary plant slaughter, so..."

He gazed at her. "I trust you." His eyes lingered on

hers for a moment, then he nodded toward the pot. "Give it lots of sun. Keep it moist but not too wet, and don't let it dry out. Let me know when it sprouts, and I'll help you transplant it."

"Okay. Sun, not too wet, not too dry. Got it." Jess already felt sad. Each time a plant died, she took it to heart. At least this time, she wouldn't have to see it since the seed was still buried in dirt.

"Well, you've got a plant to tend to, and I've got... work."

A breeze blew in through the window and tossed a wisp of Jess's hair over her face. Mark brushed it away, but his hand lingered in her hair, barely touching her head.

Jess's heart took flight. The moment was fleeting yet long enough to wonder if she would be able to take her next breath. Her lips parted, and she looked up at him. Then it happened—the kiss moment— when two people found themselves frozen in time. And in that instant, they both knew it was going to happen.

Her phone chirped in her pocket. If moments were glass, their kiss moment would lie in tiny broken sharp glints of reflected light at their feet. Jess's lips spread into a reflexive smile as she pulled her phone out of her pocket. She read the text message and made a sour face.

Mark glanced at the phone in her hand. "Everything okay?"

Startled from her thoughts, she glanced up. "Oh, yes. It's just... ugh. It's my mom reminding me about a wedding I'm trying to forget."

"Not yours, I hope."

"Ha!" Jess startled herself with her volume. She lowered her voice. "Uh, no. Proof that there's always a bright side." Her mirth faded quickly as she started to lose herself in his steady gaze. "Anyway, thank you so much for the dirt." There was more truth to her humor than she cared to admit, since the poor seedling was doomed in her care.

"It's a plant." There was a hint of disapproval in his tone.

"Shh. I'm trying not to get my hopes up. It'll just lead to heartache."

Mark shook his head, smiling. He walked to the door and said goodbye before leaving her alone.

Jess turned and looked for a sunny spot for her new pot of dirt.

THE NEXT MORNING, Jess surrendered to insomnia. She'd been up half the night. Unable to sleep, she'd finally given up and camped out on the sofa. Too tired to read, she watched three house-hunting shows until she drifted off in somebody's kitchen.

Not long after that, her daily phone alarm went off. She glanced at the time and got up. *Suck it up, buttercup. Your day off is over. Time to get back to work.*

Not yet alert, she went through her routine of putting on coffee—she was practically out—getting her favorite mug from the cabinet, and going to the window for her first Mark sighting of the day. Mark's daily walk by the sea had quickly become part of her morning routine. *All you need now are a half dozen cats and some spongy pink rollers.* She leaned her elbows on the window frame for a minute. He was late, but the coffee was ready, so she shifted priorities and turned from the window in favor of her morning brew.

She had just poured a cup when Mark knocked on the door. She knew it was Mark because at some point, she'd memorized the distinct rhythm of his knock, a fact which, even to Jess, was a little disturbing. His knock wasn't disturbing. That was fine. But she'd memorized it.

She answered the door. Mark's expression changed notably when he took in her appearance, so much so that her hand shot to her hair, and she smoothed it back. Had she brushed it at all since her shower the evening before? She must have. *Probably not.*

"What happened to you?" he asked with concern.

Jess stared. "Thank you?"

He took in a quick breath. "What I meant was, are you okay?"

"Yes. I just got up," she said, but he appeared unconvinced, as if that couldn't be enough to explain how dreadful she looked. "I'm not a morning person."

He shook his head slowly. "Good to know. I wanted to stop by and see how you were. I noticed your light on last night." He averted his eyes. "I hope that doesn't sound as creepy as it... sounds."

"Not at all." *Not nearly as creepy as my watching you on your dock every morning.*

He seemed compelled to explain. The poor man had no idea his little "I noticed your light" was just kid's play compared to her morning routine.

He cleared his throat. "It's just that our cottages kind of face each other, and at night, the lights reflect on the water, so I tend to notice—" He winced and stopped talking abruptly.

Jess cheerily assured him. "It's okay. Thanks for thinking of me."

"Well, the last thing you need is to stand here, having to listen to me rambling. Do you need anything? I'm running out to the store."

"I'm fine, thanks." She smiled, and he left. Then Jess closed the door and turned to catch her reflection in the mirror. *Ack! Well, now he's seen your natural beauty. Game over.*

A cup of coffee and a fresh change of clothes later, Jess was staring at her computer screen, having trouble getting her workday started. And she was running low on coffee. She went to the kitchen and opened the freezer, the cupboards, and the silverware drawer. That was just desperation. Her search netted two frozen diet dinners, a can of mushroom soup, and a box of uncooked spaghetti. For breakfast.

Venturing out of her lair was inevitable. She slipped on her shoes and headed out the door.

She practically tripped over a brown cardboard box. Inside was a bag of ground coffee and a muffin. Warmth filled her heart. "Mark." Jess glanced around, but Mark was long gone.

"Dammit, now I'm in love."

ELEVEN

A WEEK LATER, Mark took Jess to an indoor pool at a nearby health club. He made it clear that it wasn't an option. If she was going to live by the water, she was going to learn how to swim. Lesson one was floating. There was touching involved.

Since her fall off the pier, Jess had thought through the whole Mark thing. She gave up denying her feelings for him. She was way past that point. But he didn't have to know. She could still stick to her plan of refocusing herself to become the independent small-business mogul she intended to be. But Mark wasn't making it easy. While she tried to concentrate on floating on top of the water without sinking, she was constantly distracted by his hands on her back. The worse she did, the more Mark had to touch her to keep her afloat, which began to present a conundrum. In her weak moments, she found herself wanting to sink just so Mark would have to hold her. Fortunately, she had lucid moments that won out. She couldn't count on Mark being there the next time she found herself in water over her head, so she had ample motivation to excel in their lessons.

"How long do you think it'll take?" she asked him.

"That depends upon how good a student you are."

He'd just tapped into her overachiever issues. Now she was determined not only to swim but to excel. She had her work cut out for her since her current swimming peers were about two years old.

A few lessons in, Jess mastered the breaststroke. Many times, she had cursed the idiot who'd come up with that name. At that point in their "friendship," the names "breaststroke" and "Mark" did not need to be juxtaposed.

To commemorate Jess's breaststroke success, Mark suggested they go out for dinner and celebratory drinks. She went home to shower and change, and Mark arrived to pick her up an hour later. Her mother, with her usual perfect timing, had just called, so Jess answered the door with the phone at her ear. She waved Mark into the kitchen, pointed to a bottle of wine, and handed him a corkscrew. Brilliant man that he was, he deduced what was needed then opened and poured the wine while she tried to cut off her mother.

Jess held up a finger to Mark to signal that she would just be a minute. Then she said into the phone, "Yeah, I'll be there."

Her mother said, "If you can't find a plus-one, one of my tennis friend's son just passed the bar, and he'd love to join you."

She shut her eyes for a moment. Fully aware Mark was in earshot, Jess lowered her voice. "Well, that's lovely, but I don't need one."

"Hold on." Her voice grew muffled. "I'll have the Impertinent Pink nail polish."

"Mom?"

"Jess?" The sound quality cleared up. "Sorry. I'm at the salon getting my nails done. Now, where was I?"

Jess shook her head and hoped her mom wouldn't remember.

Her mother said, "Oh, I remember. So why don't I make the arrangements?"

"No!" Jess looked up, made eye contact with Mark, and then lowered her voice. "Mom, I've got to go. Can I call you back later?"

"That's okay. I think we're almost done here. I'll make all the arrangements."

"Arrangements? No." Was her mother trying to irk her, or was it effortless? Jess spoke in as emphatic a whisper as she could manage. "Mom, I don't need a plus-one."

"Do the math, dear. Without a plus-one, you're a zero."

"Thanks, Mom. I'll be fine." She rolled her eyes and nodded. "I know. Love you, too. Gotta go. Bye, Mom. Okay. Bye." She ended the call and set down the phone with a mortified sigh. "I am so sorry you had to hear that."

With a warm gaze, Mark handed her a glass. "She loves you."

Jess nodded and shrugged.

Mark lifted his glass. "Here's to Jess Pelletier, champion swimmer."

Jess clinked her glass against his, and they each took a sip.

Mark glanced away, appearing deep in thought, then turned back to Jess. "I couldn't help but overhear. If you need a plus-one, I'm available."

She was surprised, even tempted, but she couldn't accept his offer, even though she'd really been dreading having to go to the wedding at all—especially alone—where she would have to face her ex-fiancé, Adam. He would be there with his new girlfriend. He certainly wasn't a time waster, that one. She cringed every time she thought of him moving on so quickly. But she couldn't put Mark through all that drama.

When she didn't respond, Mark said, "I've overstepped. I just thought... Never mind."

"No! It's not that." *What is it?* She couldn't exactly tell him she was desperately trying to resist building her life around a man again. Everything was going so well. But then she thought about Adam and heaved a sigh. "My ex-fiancé is going to be there."

Mark nodded slowly. "Oh."

"Yeah." She could barely get the words out. "With a plus-one."

Mark didn't say anything. Jess figured he was probably plotting a hasty exit. Her thoughts lingered on the wedding and what it would be like. It wasn't so much about Adam. She didn't want him back. But she didn't relish the idea of sitting at one of those big, round tables all alone while everyone partnered off and went to the dance floor. Her mother was right, although she hated to admit it. She would wind up spending the evening pretending to be busy on her phone, all the while feeling like a "wallflower."

"Pardon?" Mark appeared understandably lost.

Jess inwardly cringed when she realized she'd been talking aloud. "Oh, I'm sorry. Bad habit—thinking out loud—the curse of living alone. I really need to do something about that."

"You're not a wallflower," he assured her with convincing disbelief.

Jess shook her head. "It's my mother. She said I'll feel awkward there since all of my female friends are married." She shook her head and exhaled. "So she's on the hunt to find me a date. 'Cause that won't be equally awkward. I mean why can't people imagine I could be alone and happy at the same time?" Jess hadn't meant to go off on such a sad tirade. She needed to change the subject quickly.

Mark shrugged. "I could take you. We could make an appearance, have a meal, do a little dancing." He shrugged. "Why not?"

"No." Then her mind flashed to the alternative. "Yes."

"No, yes?"

"Yes."

"You sure?"

"I think so. Why not? Okay." She nodded, convincing herself. *Have you lost your mind? Take it back! Do it now while you can.* "No, I can't ask you to do that."

"You didn't. I offered."

Her eyes narrowed as doubt filled her. "You don't know what you're in for."

"Then tell me." He seemed so calm and patient.

Jess wasn't sure whether to sigh with relief or just cower in anticipation of the wedding. But she would be doing that either way. She exhaled. "It's the perfect storm of ex-fiancé, old school friends, and parents. I mean, what could possibly go wrong?"

Mark looked kind and completely at ease. "I'll be fine."

She chuckled. "Oh, I know you'll be fine. It's me I'm worried about."

"Don't be. I have a plan."

Seeing his confidence, Jess's face brightened. "A plan? Let's hear it."

Mark smiled mischievously. "You and I will go to this wedding. When is it?"

"Saturday. In Bangor."

"Good. What's that, an hour's drive away?"

Jess tilted her head and nodded.

He gave her a quizzical look. "You don't still love him, do you?"

"No!" Her response came out a little too loudly, which prompted a startled look from Mark. But she couldn't help it if her horror was genuine. "I mean, no," she said sweetly.

He just stood there, smiling at her.

Jess licked her dry lips. "So your plan..."

"Ah, yes, the plan. You and I will go to the wedding on Saturday in Bangor." He held out his hands, as if that was all there was to it.

"That's your plan?" Jess wasn't sure what she'd expected. Maybe a fairy godmother and coach? "I'm not sure whether to feel grateful or embarrassed."

"Neither. Weddings are tough."

"Really? For guys too?" She studied him, wishing some of his nonchalance would rub off on her.

Mark was thoughtfully quiet for a moment. "Honestly? Probably not as much. But divorces suck worse, and I can tell you that from experience."

"Oh. I didn't know. How long ago?"

"Five years. Long enough to know that I'll never go through it again—either one, actually—marriage or divorce."

"Maybe this isn't such a good idea, then—going to a wedding."

"No, it's fine. As long as I'm not the groom, it's fantastic."

"Relax. My white gown's at the cleaners." That sounded presumptuous. "I mean... not that you and I—"

Mark laughed, and she relaxed and joined in. Then Mark said, "Good. Sounds like a great evening out for some food and a couple of drinks, maybe some dancing. And at some point, a couple—not us—will get married."

TWELVE

JESS WAS ready a full twenty minutes before Mark was due to pick her up for the wedding. She wore her favorite dress, the one that made her feel pretty. Whether it actually did might've been debatable, but that wasn't the point. She felt good, and she hoped she looked good. Most of all, she looked forward to being with Mark. She'd had a few days to think about how nice his offer was to accompany her. She'd also had time to ponder him and his divorce. *Hmm.* But that had nothing to do with her or their friendship. It was a really nice thing he was doing for her.

Then a thought struck her. *What will he be wearing?* She'd only seen him in worn jeans and T-shirts occasionally topped by a fleece jacket. Surely he would know how to dress for a wedding. Yes. Of course he would know. But would he care? Guys could be weird about stuff like that. She decided not to leave it to chance. She sent him a text message on the pretext of clarifying the overall dress code for the wedding.

Jess: *Forgot to mention. The wedding isn't black tie. Suit and tie would be fine.*

Mark: *ok*

Jess: *Preferably dark.*

Mark: *What color flip-flops?*

Jess stared at her phone. *Is he kidding? He's got to be kidding.*

Mark: *I'm kidding.*

JESS HEARD Mark's car and did a last-minute mirror inspection while she waited for him to knock. Then she opened the door. Stunned, she could do nothing but stare for a moment.

His eyes shone. "You look gorgeous!"

Jess rolled her eyes and blew air through her lips.

Mark sighed with regret. "I couldn't find my flip-flops. Is this okay?"

He was wearing a black suit—custom-tailored from the looks of it—a white shirt, classic black necktie, and black dress shoes. He could have walked off the set of a men's fashion magazine photo shoot.

Jess slowly nodded. "You look gorgeous too."

"I was going for handsome. Or clean. Something in that range."

"Mission accomplished." *Mission accomplished? Is that the best you can do? He looks HOT! H-O-T, HOT!*

Mark interrupted her reverie. "Shall we?"

She grabbed her wrap and her clutch and nearly forgot to lock the door... or breathe.

JESS WASN'T sure if he'd planned it, but they made it to the wedding just in time to sit down on the bride's side with no time for prewedding milling about, which was perfect. Jess's mother was first to spot them slipping into a pew toward the back, and she elbowed Jess's father, who looked back and nodded pleasantly. Then Maddie saw them and swiveled to see. What followed was a wave of head turns as every friend and acquaintance rotated in their seats to view Jess with a man—as if she and Mark were a zoo exhibit. Jess cast a nervous eye toward Mark, but he took it in stride. He cast his blue eyes on hers and smiled warmly. At first, she convinced herself that what she felt was a wave of relief. But she soon realized she was melting faster than the Wicked Witch of the West.

The head-spinning dominoes ended with Adam. Mark followed the looks he and Jess exchanged. As the wedding processional started, he maintained his steady, straight-forward gaze. "Is that him?" he whispered.

Jess kept her own gaze steady. "Yeah."

The bride entered, and everyone stood. Mark slipped his hand in Jess's and gave it a squeeze, then he held it throughout the processional.

When the ceremony was done, Maddie found her way to them, then the introductions began as people dispersed on their way to the reception. At the first opportunity, while Mark was engaged in conversation with Jess's father, her mother hooked her arm into Jess's and said under her breath, "Well, so you found a plus-one after all."

Jess grimaced. "Mom."

Kelly whispered, "So are you two an item?"

Before Jess could form a response, the men turned to them, which was a welcome distraction. They exchanged a few polite words about the weather and the wedding while people excused themselves and brushed past.

"It looks like we're blocking traffic," Jess said. "We'll catch up with you at the reception."

Her mother raised an eyebrow. "I can't wait."

Jess hooked her arm around Mark's and led him away, but not before casting a warning look at her mother, who just gazed back sweetly.

THEY'D BARELY ARRIVED at the reception when a couple of friends approached Jess. *Laura and Steve. Laura and Steve.* Jess had a deep-seated fear of forgetting names, even of people she knew very well. So she'd developed a habit of mentally repeating their names as soon as she saw them, before nervousness made her forget. So far that day, she had managed to remember everyone's name, but the day was still young.

Jess had just finished introducing Mark when Maddie joined them. She'd just opened her mouth to say something, when Steve said, "Mark Breton. *The* Mark Breton? That's why you looked so familiar!"

Confused by Steve's starstruck display, Jess turned toward Mark to see if his reaction might shed any light.

Mark gave Steve a modest smile.

Steve turned to Laura. "This is Mark Breton."

Laura responded with a confused look. "So I've heard."

Steve stared intently at Jess. "Why didn't you tell us you were dating Mark Breton?"

"I..." Jess began to mentally unpack what was happening. First of all, "dating" wasn't exactly what was going on. Next, why would she have told Steve or anyone else? It hadn't come up in conversation because they hadn't had any. She cast a nervous glance at Mark, but he appeared too uncomfortable to notice.

Steve tended to be a little on the loud side, so Jess hadn't really been fazed by his volume until he drew a small crowd of friends, Adam included. Jess gave her ex a polite nod and smile, but before they could speak, Steve exclaimed, "Dude!" Steve had been on the debate team throughout high school and college, and now he was in sales. He knew how to work a crowd and was holding court with a beer in his hand. Knowing Steve, Jess suspected it wasn't his first. "This is Mark Breton, Olympic hopeful. God, that was... what... junior year in high school?"

"A long time ago." Mark seemed patient and gracious, but Jess saw a dark light in his eyes that she hadn't seen before.

"This guy did it all—freestyle, butterfly, and the breaststroke." He winked and elbowed Jess. "Of course, you'd know all about that."

Jess's jaw dropped.

Mark put his hand on Jess's back.

She was just about to make an excuse and a hasty exit when Steve shook his head. "Shame about the accident."

Jess studied Mark. His eyes flickered with pain, but he took it in stride.

"I am dying of thirst," she quickly said. "Would

you excuse us? We'll catch up with you later." As they walked away, Jess muttered, "Unless we can avoid it."

As they worked their way over to the bar, Jess wracked her brain, trying to remember if Mark had ever talked about his past. But she couldn't have forgotten his mentioning something like the Olympics. Mark had mentioned an accident on prom night, but that was barely in passing. *Olympics?* That was a pretty huge part of his past to leave out. But the look on his face when Steve had brought it up made it clear that it wasn't something to discuss at the moment. So she was surprised when Mark took her hand and led her out to a secluded corner of the garden.

"I wasn't trying to hide it from you. I've just put that part of my life behind me. And I liked having you not know and just like me for myself."

The way he could barely look at her made it clear there was pain behind his stoic facade. "Okay. You don't owe me an explanation."

"I'll tell you about it sometime, just not here. Not tonight."

Jess nodded.

But Mark was the one who couldn't quite let it go. "I knew you'd have found out at some point. But I liked how things were with us. No baggage. Just us."

Jess tried to ease the tension. "There's nothing like a wedding to shine a spotlight on baggage."

"Well, this is mine. I swam. It was my life, and it was going to be my career. Swimming, broadcasting. I had plans, and nothing could stop me. I was driven, and it looked like it was going to happen. Prom night came. We rented a limo. We did everything right. But the other car didn't. We were T-boned in an intersection. My shoulder was crushed. End of story."

"I'm so sorry."

"That was ten, no, eleven years ago. I didn't think anyone here would remember."

"Steve was on the swim team, so I think he followed the sport pretty closely." Jess wished she could make the whole uncomfortable situation go away. Mark had saved her from a nightmare, only for it to bring on his own. But she couldn't make it go away any more than she could undo the past. "Let's go. I've made my appearance. We're good."

Mark gazed into her eyes, then he shook his head slowly. "Come here." He hooked his arm about her waist and drew her to him, then he kissed her on the forehead. "Not until we do the Macarena. I've lived for that moment." With a mischievous twinkle, he took her hand then went in search of their table.

Over dinner, Mark managed to field questions from those at their table about swimming then artfully guided the subject away from himself. Over dessert, he turned to Jess, and they talked to one another. If anyone else was still there at the table, the two of them seemed unaware.

"I can't see you as the competitive type," Jess said.

His eyes widened. "Oh, I was."

"But you seem so laid-back."

"Yeah? Maybe so, but back then, it was all about swimming. But when the accident happened, I had nowhere to go, so I guess I stood still. After I recovered from the shoulder replacement, I gave up. Swimming was over competitively. So the way I coped was to give up. I stayed home, avoided people, didn't work."

"It's understandable." Jess studied his face and tried to imagine him back then.

Mark heaved a sigh. "I didn't know what to do after that. Swimming was all I ever wanted or knew how to do. I had no other talents or skills. For a while, I lived off the competition prize money I'd saved up in the bank. It was supposed to go toward my training, but I didn't need it for that anymore. Then I fell into doing odd jobs for my aunt. I think she made some of them up just to get me out of the house. But it worked, and it helped. I did gardening and landscaping, and I helped at the office. She saved me from myself—she and my grandparents. They left me some money, so I didn't have to worry about that. The original plan was for it to help me financially so I could pursue my Olympic dream. But when that was over, at least it bought me time to wallow in the hand fate had dealt me."

Jess put her hand on his.

"Sorry. Long, boring story."

She squeezed his hand. "No."

"I'm okay now. I've found ways to fill in the time between the odd jobs. As part of my inheritance, my grandfather left me his old, worn-out yacht, and I've made it a project. I've got enough for food and shelter, and I'm content with my life."

Jess debated whether to bring up the fact that she'd watched him. "I've seen you in the mornings on the dock."

His eyes flicked toward hers, and a smile came and went. "Yeah. I used to swim in the mornings when the sun was just coming up. So sometimes I like to go out in the still morning air and look out at the water. I can still feel it, every stroke propelling me forward until I'm one with the water. And everything works, and I'm free. There's a sort of weightless state that you reach when everything is in balance." The light of better days shone in his eyes. "That's why I did it. It wasn't the glory." He scoffed. "Winning is great, but when it's just you and water, and everything is smooth and right, it's euphoric, like being in love."

He had mentioned divorce, so she couldn't help but be curious. "When did you get married?"

Mark nodded and rolled his eyes. "We were young. All hormones, no brains. As soon as we'd both turned eighteen, we eloped. It was crazy. Then when things went south after the accident, she bailed."

"Wow. That was a lot for you all at once."

His pleasant expression was beginning to look a bit forced. "Tell me about it. I put all of that away. Like it's locked in a room. And I don't go there often."

Jess ached for him. "Except when you're dragged to a wedding where people recognize you."

"Yeah, well, it happens. Not often, though, anymore. I guess it's a perk of living in a small town. Everyone knows about it, so no one talks about it anymore."

They were interrupted by speeches and toasts, then the dancing began.

"Do you swim still?" Jess asked. "Ever? I mean, you look like everything works."

His eyes flashed. "I had a shoulder replacement. It works okay. And—bonus—it can predict the weather." His smile faded. "I confine my self-indulgence to those dawns on the dock. Sometimes I get into the water, but it's gone. My stroke's clumsy. All that's left is a painful reminder that that part of my life is gone. So I tend to avoid it."

Jess fought the urge to keep saying she was sorry. It

would just make matters worse. All this while, he'd been carrying such a huge loss around with him.

"It's okay," Mark said. "I've moved on. It's a little like waking up from a dream that you can't go back to. So you just have to get up and get on with your day." He took a deep breath. "And have new dreams, like dancing with you." He stood and held his hand out as the music changed to a ballad.

Jess told herself it was the two glasses of wine that she'd had, but she knew she could no longer ignore how she felt about Mark. He held her close, and every touch amplified her senses. His hand lightly pressed against her back, and his other hand held hers. They drew closer to each other as if they couldn't do anything else. It was electric. He had to feel it too. As the final chord played, they were poised cheek to cheek. Mark turned slightly and brushed his lips over her cheek, and she leaned into him. Like a thirst, she had to touch her lips to his. And they kissed. It was soft and over too soon, then they both pulled away and looked at one another with the realization that there was something between them. They both knew it. Mark's eyes were as honest and open as she felt. It seemed like everything in the world—the disorder, chaos, painful memories of the past—all of it suddenly settled into place. And they had each other.

Jess saw a couple of friends heading toward them.

No, don't ruin this moment. It's perfect. She turned to Mark. "Excuse me. I'll be right back."

He smiled with the same light in his eyes that she felt coming from hers. He gave her hand a squeeze then released it.

She escaped to the bathroom and emerged two minutes later with her wild emotions nearly quelled. Then her peace was shattered by familiar voices. Bethany, Megan, and Ashley. They'd been friends all through college, and they'd had a lot of fun. Jess liked them, but they were in different places now. Not only was Jess the last one of their group who was single, but her friends' lives were centered on babies. Two of them balanced successful careers, while the third worked at home, raising a family. Maybe that was what was going on—all the children were with grandparents or sitters, which gave Jess's friends a rare chance to regress to their past college ways. They were in full-on party mode.

"So, Jess, when's the wedding?" Bethany asked.

Jess observed at the giggling group. "Calm yourselves. It's a date."

Megan gave Jess an approving look. "He is perfect. If I were you, I'd get to work closing that deal. Time to start planning your future."

You don't even know him! Granted, he is perfect,

but that doesn't mean I'm going to discuss our future with you.

"My future's just fine."

The three women stared blankly at her, which may have lasted only a moment or two, but the silence was too much to bear. Jess felt the need to explain. "I'm enjoying my life now. I like living alone, and I'm building my business. Frankly, I'd be just fine staying single the rest of my life."

Megan peered at her. "Life without a man—ever?"

Ashley gave Megan a chastising look. "Don't be so heteronormative." She turned back to Jess and shook her head apologetically.

Bethany seemed stuck on an earlier thought. "You'd rather be single? No sex?"

That put Jess on the defensive. "I didn't say that. I can have an occasional fling." Bethany's mouth was agape, while the others appeared a bit envious.

Mark appeared at her side and leaned close to her ear. "You don't strike me as the occasional-fling type."

Jess didn't just hear his voice. She could feel it reverberate down to her soul. Startled, she turned. He was beaming. She had no idea what her friends did or said after that. Mark made some sort of excuse then led her by the hand to the dance floor. Halfway through the song, his lips brushed her ear as he spoke. "Occasional fling?"

Jess wasn't sure if she could breathe, let alone reply. He managed to cut through all of her usual layers of armor. He seemed to want some sort of answer. She could make something up, but he would know. Or maybe, with him, she couldn't even make things up. She couldn't seem to be anything but honest with him. "I just... didn't want them to feel sorry for me."

He pulled away enough to look into her eyes in disbelief. Everything seemed to stop. They might have stopped dancing. Jess wasn't aware of anything except Mark and the way he was looking at her. "What if you didn't have an occasional fling? What if you and I meant something to each other?"

Her lips parted. She managed to whisper a feeble, "Okay."

Then he kissed her. His lips felt full and soft, and she melted into his arms. She was suddenly aware of a bright light. *Oh, wow. He just kissed me so well, I might be having an out-of-body experience, which would be a waste under the circumstances.*

As if awakening, Mark looked around, and Jess followed suit.

Some genius whom Jess couldn't see behind the blinding light had taken control of the spotlight and shined it on them. The guests applauded, and Jess caught sight of her girlfriends eyeing her gleefully. Had she ever really been close to them? It seemed so long ago. But there they were. Jess averted her eyes. They could laugh, but she didn't have to look at them.

Then she saw Adam. He stared at Jess while his date stared at him. Jess felt a pang of emotion. It was like finding an old photo and remembering a moment together, separate from anything before or after. But it was only a long-ago memory. Her feelings for Adam were gone. And it struck her. She was free. Feeling euphoric, she turned to Mark.

His eyes glowed with affection. "Had enough?"

She was hoping that he meant the wedding, because she hadn't had nearly enough of that kiss. "I just need to say a few quick goodbyes."

THIRTEEN

AN HOUR LATER, they drove past the sign for the township of Applecross Cove, and Jess felt like she had come home. Moving into a new house was one thing, but home was another. She wondered when her new town had become home. She suspected Mark had something to do with it.

"I've got some champagne in the fridge," he said. "Care to join me?"

"I'd love to." *How divine.* She felt like she'd just dropped into an Audrey Hepburn movie, dashing about in a sports car—well, Mark drove a pickup— where they said things like "darling" and "wildly romantic." She was soaring on one of those white puffy clouds that sailed over the ocean on a warm summer day.

Mark held Jess's hand on and off for the whole ride

home. How he managed to make her heart pound just by holding her hand was beyond logic. In truth, she'd had that reaction to him the whole evening and in the days since she'd met him. It all seemed so unreal. Mark was different, though. He was more thoughtful and kinder than any man had ever been to her. He had overcome heartbreaking disappointment and risen above it. And he happened to be tall and strapping, with clear blue eyes, messy brown hair, and arms that felt so good wrapped around her.

When they arrived at Mark's cottage, he got out and walked around the car to open her door. As soon as he did, they flew into each other's arms and kissed. Once his lips parted, she was lost. She couldn't get close enough. Neither could he.

With no warning, he pulled away and clasped her hand. "Let's go inside before the neighbors make popcorn and gawk out their windows."

Jess laughed.

They were both still laughing as they ran up the walkway and inside the door. Jess looked around at the wide-planked wood floors and massive stone fireplace. Plenty of large windows must have had amazing views in the daylight. "I've never been in here. I love it!"

He pulled her into his arms. "I love you."

Jess stiffened and took a step back. All she could do was stare wide-eyed at him.

He appeared almost as stunned as she did. "I'm sorry. That just came out."

"Mark." A sudden wave of emotion rose from nowhere. She was breathless as she lifted her eyes to meet his.

He slowly removed his hands from her shoulders and took a step back. "Jess, I know. It's way too soon for that." He glanced toward the kitchen. "Forget what I said. Let's not waste the champagne. If I promise not to speak, would you sit on the deck and have some champagne to cap off a nice day?"

Jess couldn't speak.

"Right. I'll go open the bottle." He turned to head for the kitchen.

Jess reached out, yanked him back, then grabbed his lapels and pulled him close. She planted a hard kiss on his lips. Then she blurted out, "I love you too."

But the reaction she got wasn't what she'd expected. He took hold of her shoulders and held her at bay. "Jess, weddings make people... emotional. It brings out things that would otherwise never see the light of day."

"You didn't mean it?"

His eyebrows drew together, and he peered into her eyes. "I fell a little in love when I brought you your key, and I've been falling for you ever since."

"This wasn't the plan. But I love you too. I didn't think I could—or even wanted to love again."

"Wait." He said it so firmly, she thought something might be wrong. But his mouth spread into a smile as he stepped closer and drew her against him. "Say that first part again."

"This wasn't the plan?"

His eyes shone. "No, the other part."

"I love you too."

"That's the one." His blissful look faded. "Are you sure?"

She gazed into those blue eyes that she loved. "Yes."

"That's all I need to know. We can talk in the morning." He slipped his arms around her waist and touched his forehead to hers. "Over breakfast, I hope."

They let go of everything they'd been holding back, wanting only to be closer with nothing between them. As they worked their way through the hall, Jess let her clutch and wrap drop to the floor. They kicked their shoes off one by one then paused to lean on the doorframe while Jess fumbled her way down Mark's shirt and unfastened the buttons. He unzipped her dress, wrapped his arms about her, and lifted her up off of her feet while he kissed her.

They kissed as he carried her into the great room, then

he leaned against the banister and kissed her again. With a dismissive glance up the stairs toward his bedroom, he instead led her to the much closer dining room table. Mark lifted Jess onto the edge of the table and planted a kiss on her lips that made Jess nearly swoon while she unzipped his trousers. He yanked his shirttails free then grasped the hem of her dress and slid it up her thigh.

Jess let out a surprised "Oh!" as she leaned back on Mark's laptop. With one swipe, he shoved it out of the way. When the display lit up, Jess glanced over and froze.

Unaware anything was wrong, Mark brushed his mouth over her earlobe on the way to her mouth, but Jess put her palms on his chest. "Wait. Stop."

Mark leaned back and stared at her. "What's wrong?"

"What's that?" she asked softly. "Never mind. I know what it is. Stock tables and ticker symbols."

"Yeah." Mark smiled. "We can talk about stocks in the morning. It's the weekend. The S&P isn't going anywhere." He leaned closer to kiss her, but she gently pushed him away.

"You play the stock market."

"Yeah, I guess." He peered at her with increasing confusion. "Jess? What is it?"

"You're a day trader."

"I wouldn't say that. I trade stocks. I invest. People do it all over the world."

Jess glanced about as though she were lost. "But I didn't know you did."

"Jess?"

"I'm sorry. I can't." She peered into his eyes. "I've gotta go. Sorry."

Mark stepped back, giving her room to stand up. Jess tried to zip up her dress, but it got stuck, and she cursed. Mark zipped it up for her.

With a frustrated thank-you, Jess rushed toward the door. She tried to slip on her shoes but gave up and scooped them up along with her wrap and clutch as she rushed out of the cottage.

Mark followed and called out after her from the doorway. "Jess, let me walk you home."

"I can walk," she called back as she scurried down the path.

"But it's dark."

"Flashlight app," she said, hoping he couldn't hear that she was crying.

She managed to make it back home, through the door, and onto her sofa. Then she buried her face in a pillow.

FOURTEEN

IT WAS DAWN, and Jess was awake. The clouds hovered over the horizon like smoke over the faint glow of embers. She was making coffee when she glanced down at Mark's pot of dirt on the windowsill. *Great. Just what I need—a reminder of how I kill growing things—plants and relationships.* Jess picked up the pot and set it outside on the edge of the deck, where she wouldn't have to see it.

Last night was exactly what she'd worked so hard to avoid. If she'd kept to her plan, she would have woken up feeling fine. There might have been a little ego bruising at the wedding, but she would have come home and recovered. Life would go on. But with each step she took toward a relationship, she gave away that much more control. Now she'd left herself open to hurt.

It was human nature for people to hide things away until it was too late. There was always some sort of surprise. Which was why she wanted to take time off from relationships until she was strong enough to cope with the unexpected—and there was always something unexpected. She didn't blame Mark. There was no reason for him to have told her. No, she blamed herself.

Determined not to let this whole Mark thing derail her, she went to the fitness club pool to swim laps. At least that was one positive thing that had come from the situation. She had learned how to swim. She'd joined a health club with an indoor pool, where she practiced almost daily. She had recently worked up to swimming laps. That morning, she expected it to get her mind off her troubles, but it only gave her more time to think.

Last night had been a dream and a nightmare all wrapped up in one evening. She and Mark had both said the L word only to break up before midnight. She felt like some sort of surly Cinderella whose prince had taken up the wrong hobbies. Her fairy godmother must be so pissed. After all that wand-waving, Jess had rejected a perfectly suitable prince. That was not how it was supposed to work.

Jess had to have broken some sort of speed record for dating, not to mention heartbreak. She kept seeing the look on Mark's face when she'd left. He'd been dismayed and bewildered. What else could he have been? Jess barely understood it herself. It had all happened so quickly. She'd seen the stock charts and symbols, and something inside her had shut down. Her fight-or-flight instincts had kicked in, and all she'd been able to do was get out of that place. Nothing else had mattered, least of all Mark's feelings. She may have been blind to them then, but now she couldn't escape them. She'd blindsided him. With one swift, sudden act, she'd struck a blow from which he might not ever recover.

MADDIE SIGHED on the other end of the line. "Aren't you being a little dramatic?"

"No, Maddie. You weren't there. It was awful." Jess walked from her car to her cottage and struggled to hang up her swimsuit on the shower rod while holding the phone. Then with similar awkwardness, she poured herself a glass of water and opened the screen door leading out to the deck. The screen closed behind her with a slam.

"What was that?" Maddie shouted.

Jess moved the phone away from her ear. "The door."

"Phew! I thought maybe he'd come after you with—"

"A screen door? Right. In a fit of passion, he slammed his fist through the screen and let the flies in. That'll show me."

Maddie seemed unfazed by her attempt at humor. "Hey, black flies are no joke."

"Neither is this." Jess leaned back and sighed. "This isn't quite as helpful as I thought it would be."

"Yeah? Wow. That really puts a dent in my grief counseling career plans."

Jess smirked. "Probably for the best."

"Which brings us back to you. Maybe it's for the best."

That wasn't what Jess wanted to hear.

"You're pouting, aren't you?" Maddie asked.

"No comment."

"Which means yes. So, Option B: maybe it wasn't as bad as you think."

Jess blew air through her lips.

"Excuse you," Maddie said. "Now, what if he just thinks that you're shy? Or you thought you'd left the oven on and had to rush home to check? Or you didn't want him to see you in your shapewear."

Jess wrinkled her face. "That's the best you can do? I'm falling apart here."

"Okay, okay. How 'bout this? Talk to him."

"What?" Jess looked around as though she might be able to pull a better plan out of the air.

"Yeah. That's my best advice. Talk to him. Tell him the truth."

"That's crazy." Jess couldn't help but smile through her misery.

"I know! And guess what? It might work."

Jess stared over at Mark's cottage and sighed. "I guess."

"Which means you'll do it?"

"Yes."

"Good."

"Thanks, Maddie."

"Stay in touch."

Jess laughed. "I'll try." She hung up and stared out at the sea. She did at least owe Mark the truth. Only a jerk would walk away without letting him know it wasn't really his fault. They needed closure. Otherwise, it would only make things awkward when they ran into one another, which they would. It was only a matter of time in a small town like Applecross Cove. No, she wouldn't leave him like that. The least she could do was be honest and fair. They were grown-ups. And he deserved more. So it was settled—or it would be soon enough.

WITH HER PULSE RACING NERVOUSLY, Jess walked up to Mark's door with a cardboard tray of coffee and muffins and rang the doorbell. Mark opened the door, wearing a T-shirt and sweats. He looked good enough to make her forget everything, sink into his arms, and run her fingers through his tousled hair. Almost.

He stared at her blankly without saying anything.

"I was hoping we could talk."

He hesitated long enough for Jess to wish the ground would swallow her up while she waited for him to say no and close the door in her face. To her surprise, he didn't.

As if resigning himself to the inevitable, Mark stepped back and stretched out his arm in silent invitation. They went out to the deck, which looked out at the mist rising up from the water, revealing glimpses of lobster boats through its gauzy haze.

Jess took a sip of her coffee. "Adam was a day trader."

From the look on his face, he didn't really care.

But she'd started and would not be deterred. "When I met Adam, he was a stockbroker. He was bright and aggressively dedicated to work. He liked nice things, fine restaurants, and he swept me off my feet."

"Look, Jess—"

"No. I need you to know so you'll understand."

Mark leaned back and folded his arms.

"We were together for two years before he proposed. I was falling into step with my friends with their weddings and babies. I felt like I had finally joined the club. Then one day, with no warning, he left work and never went back. He became a day trader, spending his days and much of his nights trading stocks. He seemed happy at first, working at home in his bathrobe. But then he began losing sleep. When the market was closed, he was studying it. And he changed. He didn't have time to go out. We barely saw each other, and when we did, he seemed like a man possessed, an empty shell."

"Jess, I don't see what this has to do with me."

"It's not you."

He seemed confused.

"What's happened between us is on me."

"That's what kind people say to avoid the obvious. Or to avoid their own guilt."

Jess wanted to argue the point, but she couldn't. He was right. She felt guilty, but there was so much more. She went on. "I'll never know what happened to Adam exactly, whether it was one huge loss or a series of small ones. It doesn't matter. He lost it. Everything. His savings. He borrowed against his retirement. He got a second mortgage on his home. He lost everything except his home. But I didn't know any of this until later. He moved in with me. He said it was to save money for the wedding, but I later found out that he'd rented his home out so he could make the payments. Then the day came to close on the house—our dream house."

Jess's voice wavered. She took a deep breath and tried to pull it together. "I don't know what he thought was going to happen. I guess he thought he'd get lucky at the last minute and somehow it all would work out. But I was dressed and ready to walk out the door to go close on our house when he stopped me." Jess shut her eyes for a moment, overwhelmed by the memory. "He broke down crying. He'd spent our down payment. A hundred thousand dollars—half of it mine—gone. It was gone, and there was nothing I could do except kick myself for having trusted him with my money. But we were going to get married. I should have been able to trust him."

Jess sipped her coffee and stared through the haze at the harbor. "He had—has—an addiction to stock trading. For him, it's like gambling. It ruined our finances and ended our relationship. It'll take me years to recoup my share of what he lost. I was devastated. That's why I moved here—to get away. My old life was too damaged to fix. If I couldn't have my life back, at least I could have some control. So I came here to start over. I wasn't looking for a relationship, but I met you. And then last night..."

"You saw my computer."

She nodded. "And it all came back. I was back where my life fell apart."

Mark leaned forward and took in a breath, but before he could speak, Jess cut in. "I'm not judging or asking you to change. It's my problem. I can't even look at a ticker symbol without feeling sick. I can't help it."

Mark looked away with a mixture of annoyance and incomprehension. "I've got some investments. I keep a close eye, but I'm not a day trader. I'm a blue-chip, Dow 30 kinda guy. I might pick up a few shares in an IPO here and there just for fun. And I've got a couple of stocks I invest in because I believe in what the companies are doing. But I mainly just set and forget."

Jess considered his words, but she couldn't get past it. "Adam seemed like he had it under control too."

Mark got up, went to the deck rail, and stared for a long while.

Jess couldn't take the silence. "I'm sorry."

She'd barely gotten the words out when, jaw clenched, Mark quietly said, "I'm not Adam."

Jess flinched. She'd never seen him so angry. And so quiet. She almost wished he would yell. Then she would know where things stood.

Mark turned back toward her and leaned on the deck, but he barely made eye contact. "I'm sorry that happened to you. But it has nothing to do with me. You know me, and you should be able to see that." He fixed narrowed eyes on hers. "You should trust me." He shook his head in disgust and stared off into the distance, his arms folded.

The silence that followed seemed like forever to Jess. But she didn't know what else to say. Then they both started speaking at once. Jess shook her head. "Go ahead." For a brief moment, she thought they might be able to work things out somehow. But she knew that was impossible when she was the one who couldn't move. She couldn't risk it. She hadn't even come close to putting her life back together from the last failed relationship.

Mark came over and sat back down in the chair next to hers. "We both said things last night."

How could she forget? They'd both said that they loved each other just before it had all fallen apart.

Mark spoke in deep, measured tones. "We both got out over our skis."

Jess's stomach sank. Sure, she had some issues, but she had not spoken lightly of love. She had only said those words to one man before. What she felt for Mark was real. No matter how hard she'd tried to protect herself from it, she'd fallen in love. The stock trading issue was huge, but she believed what Mark told her. He didn't have a problem like Adam's. The problem was hers. She'd been burned, and her feelings were real. She couldn't simply will them away. But she had to find some way through this.

In that moment, she realized that her love for Mark had become something more than she'd ever imagined love could be. She had crossed over a line to a sort of love in which nothing else mattered. She loved him completely, no matter what might come between them. There could be no other option. She loved him too much to give up. "Look, I know I have a problem with stocks."

His eyes flashed. "No. You have a problem with trust."

She nodded. "Okay, fair enough. But I want to work through it."

His blue eyes settled on hers, cold as ice. "Good. I think you should. Just not with me." He stood up and started toward the door.

"Mark—"

"I've been here before. I don't want this kind of love."

"What's that supposed to mean?"

"Love that withers at the first sign of a storm."

"Can't we just take a step back?" Jess asked.

Mark regarded her wearily then shook his head. "C'mon, I'll walk you out."

Outside, Jess passed by Wanda, who stopped in her tracks while Jess gave her a hasty hello through her tears and kept going.

Mark leaned against the doorframe and folded his arms as his aunt looked at him quizzically. "Don't ask."

Wanda leveled a wry look over her glasses as Mark stepped aside so she could enter. She went straight to the coffeepot. "You realize I gave her that cottage at a discount."

Mark's forehead creased. "First, why? And second, what does that have to do with anything?"

"I like her. You need someone like that in your life."

Mark pulled a mug down from the cabinet and poured coffee for his aunt. They sat down at the great room table, which was situated by a huge window that framed a spectacular view of the coast. "You're taking your real estate business to a whole new level here, aren't you?" he asked.

Wanda's eyes twinkled. "Well, someone has to. And your parents are too busy basking in the sun in their Florida home."

Mark tried to be patient, but he wasn't exactly in the mood for this conversation. "Do I look like I can't get a date?"

Wanda's eyes softened. "You look like you've just lost one."

Mark stared at the table. "Yeah, more or less."

"I'm guessing more?"

He regarded her with as much patience as he could muster. "Aunt Wanda, I'm fine. I like my life. It's simple. No complications."

Wanda gazed at him. "Oh, really? I thought I saw a complication running down the walkway just now."

"Yeah." Mark stared at his hands then glanced up and forced a smile. "So, how are you?"

Wanda didn't force the issue. "I want to show you a house I was thinking of buying. It would make a fantastic vacation rental, or a house flip. I'm not sure yet. I want you to see it. I thought we might fix it up and split the proceeds."

Mark grinned. "Sure." By "we," she meant Mark. But she was willing to risk her money. All he had to do was the work, and she gave him a large piece of the profits.

Wanda said brightly, "Good! Shall we go take a look?"

"Why not?"

JESS SPENT the next few days trying to pour herself into work, but her heart ached. She blamed herself. She had started out trying to move slowly. Mark was such a good friend, but her heart had other ideas. Once her feelings had taken over, there was no turning back. Had she taken the time and kept her feelings at bay, she would have found out about his stock market trading in time to protect herself—and him. But she hadn't. They'd both jumped off a ledge, thinking they were falling in love. Instead, there was just a big pile of pain, and they'd both landed in it.

She'd seen it coming, and she had tried to resist. But he was just so good-looking.

Good-looking doesn't mean good for you. Maybe I should put that on a fridge magnet and read it next time I have feelings.

FIFTEEN

A WEEK PASSED, and Jess found it surprisingly easy to avoid running into Mark—as long as she stayed in her house and led the life of a Cistercian monk. *Aren't they the ones who make ale?* She could learn to adapt to the lifestyle.

In the past few days, she'd developed an effective routine, saving shopping trips for late at night. She would arrive at the grocery store just before closing and skulk around until the last shopper was gone. Then she would grab an armful of frozen diet entrees and a few pints of ice cream before making a mad dash to the self-serve register. Mornings remained roughly the same with a coffee on the deck, where she surreptitiously sought Mark sightings down by the water—and failed.

She was staring outside one bright morning when the phone rang. It was Wanda calling with a business proposition she wished to discuss. She preferred meeting in person, so they made arrangements to meet at The Bean Counter. Anyplace was fine as long as it wasn't Mark's favorite hangout, Cal's Place.

Two hours later, Jess and Wanda were sitting and drinking coffee, talking about Wanda's real estate website. Jess was thrilled to be able to help. Wanda's website currently looked like a time capsule from an era gone by, when people connected to the Internet via dial-up. Jess and Wanda talked through what Wanda needed and wanted, and Jess said she would email her landlady some sample themes to see what she liked best. The meeting went well, and Jess looked forward to working with Wanda. She liked the older woman, and the feeling seemed to be mutual.

Jess was feeling good about the new project, and ideas were flowing. Then the bell tinged against the coffee shop door, and Mark walked in.

The place was so small, they couldn't avoid seeing each other, but Wanda still waved to make sure he didn't miss them. He had no choice but to walk over to their table.

Wanda glanced from Mark to Jess, then said, "Hi, Mark."

Mark lifted an eyebrow. "Aunt Wanda." Out of a strained sense of courtesy, he said, "Jess."

"Hi." He looked good, but he always looked good.

His eyes darted away, and he turned to Wanda with a halfhearted gesture toward the window. "I saw your car outside, so I came in to say hello." His eyes flicked toward Jess.

Looking down, Jess closed her laptop and slipped it into her bag. "Well, Wanda, I think I've got what I need here to get started. I'm looking forward to working together. I'll head home now to work up some ideas and get back to you sometime tomorrow. Have a great afternoon." Jess stood and mumbled, "Bye, Mark." Then she shrugged her bag over her shoulder and left.

MARK WATCHED Jess walk through the door then turned to Wanda and put his hand on the back of the chair Jess had just vacated. "Mind?"

"Not at all."

He flagged down a server and ordered some coffee then glanced toward the front window and watched Jess walk past. With a narrow-eyed look at his aunt, he sat down to join her. "How did you manage that?"

"What?"

"This. A chance meeting with Jess."

Wanda lifted her eyebrows. "You give me too much credit."

He found that hard to believe. "It feels like a setup."

Wanda narrowed her eyes. "I haven't mastered mind reading yet. Actually, Jess and I had plans to meet here for business. I don't recall sending out invitations."

He sighed and shook his head. "Sorry."

With her point made, Wanda dismissed Mark's apology gently. "Not that I wouldn't if I could. It's not easy to see two people I care for in such obvious pain. But this is between you and Jess. I couldn't fix this if I tried."

"There is no 'this.'" He glanced up as his coffee arrived and thanked the server. Then he returned his attention to Wanda.

Her eyes softened. "So I see."

With a rueful smile, Mark shook his head. The sympathy in Wanda's eyes was almost too much to bear.

Wanda exhaled. "Let's talk house renovations."

MARK VISITED the new house project with Wanda then went to see about pulling permits. After that, he made some phone calls to line up a carpenter, electrician, plumber, drywaller, and painter. Once that was done, it was lunchtime, so he stopped in at Cal's. He'd missed the rush, which was just fine with him. He found himself increasingly craving quiet so he could get lost in his thoughts.

From his favorite table, Mark gazed out at the pier and finished his chowder and lobster roll. The typical sparse midweek collection of shoulder-season visitors were on their leisurely strolls past the shops and down the pier.

"Looking for someone out there?" Cal wiped his hands on his apron and sat down facing Mark.

Mark frowned at his friend.

Cal lifted his eyebrows knowingly. "You looked pretty intense. I know we've got great views here, but it's not like it's the first time you've seen them."

"I was thinking."

Cals eyes lit up. "Well, that explains it. Hard work for you, huh?"

Mark stared blankly.

Cal stared back. "Wow. You're like the lonely-hearts poster adult." He held out his hands as if he were framing a shot. "This is your brain on love." He waited for laughter, but Mark didn't respond. "Nothing? I don't know what she did to you, but you're no damn fun anymore." He slapped his palms on the table. "I know what. We need to go fishing. That'll cure you. Fish and beer. Mother Nature's therapists."

"Sure, fishing," Mark muttered abstractedly.

Cal proceeded to make plans, but Mark barely listened. After a few unanswered questions, Cal threw up his hands. "That's it!"

Mark glanced up, surprised.

"You need help, and Dr. Cal's gonna give it to you. Tell me something."

Mark stared and waited.

"Do you love her? I mean, we're talking about Jess, right? 'Cause if you've already got someone new, I'm gonna stop pitying you and start taking notes."

Mark made no effort to hide his annoyance. "Who else would it be?"

"I'll take that as a yes. Does she love you?"

"She said that she did," Mark muttered.

Cal leaned back and folded his arms. "Okay. So you love her. She loves you. One plus one equals two. That was easy."

Mark leveled a look that was just barely patient. "You'd think."

Cal puffed out his chest. "Let me tell you about women."

Mark blew out a breath. "This oughta be good."

"It's usually something you did, like pee on the toilet seat, spit chewing tobacco in her heirloom teacup, or hang your underpants over the hand towel rack, and then she washes her face and dries herself with them."

Cal whistled. "Word to the wise, do not ever do that. Talk about overreacting!"

"Can't imagine why you've been married three times."

"But divorced only two!" Cal hastened to add.

Mark couldn't help but smile.

"So," Cal continued, "what you do is learn how to do damage control. Take it from me. I'm a pro. Now, I've worked out a sliding scale of preemptive penance that'll get your butt out of a sling. Level one: the knee-pad shuffle. This is for things like her being pissed because you didn't rinse the dishes before you put them in the dishwasher. Which, by the way, don't even ask why. It'll just escalate things to the next level. So just shut up, get down on your knees, and grovel. Then rinse the damn dishes and offer to watch one of those movies with babes in bonnets, and you're usually off the hook.

"Level two: the man-cave mambo. Now, the man cave is the twenty-first-century version of the doghouse, tricked out because we've evolved. To be honest, there's not always a lot of incentive to get out of the man cave, but sooner or later, you'll want to crawl back into bed, and you don't want her mad at you then. So this is all about planning ahead. When in doubt, just say yes. In your case, this means say yes to the Jess."

Mark looked at Cal with pinched eyebrows and wonder. The fact that they'd grown up together in the same town, with the same friends, and at the same school should have put the question of nature or nurture to rest.

Cal managed to coax a few smiles out of Mark, which only seemed to encourage him more. "Level three, as I've already alluded to, is the butt-in-sling sidestep. If you've really screwed up—even if you haven't, but she's pissed about something—go out for a drive and don't even think about coming back without flowers. I don't get it. I mean, it's not like I couldn't pull some out of the garden. Just between you and me, I did once. But I tell you, it works. A nice clump of flowers rubber-banded in a cellophane cone, and it's magic. I guess I kinda get it. A six-pack of beer would do the same thing for me. But if you can find a woman who'll go out and buy that or anything else after a fight, marry that girl."

"Woman."

Cal shrugged. "Right."

He paused, and Mark couldn't resist. "What about level four?" He did his best to look serious.

Cal looked like he'd seen a ghost. "Bro, you do not want to go there."

Mark had to admit, Cal had piqued his interest.

"Let's just say, you might as well go straight out

and find a second job, 'cause whatever it is, it'll cost you." Cal stared at Mark intently. "So, level four is the cower and cash out." He lifted his eyebrows and nodded.

Mark had no idea what Cal was talking about.

"Remember that bathroom renovation two years ago?"

"Yeah."

Cal shrugged. "Cower and cash out."

Mark couldn't help but smile. "Must've been hard to part with that tangerine toilet and tub."

"I know, right? But that's not the point. Doesn't matter if you've got a perfectly functional bathroom. There's always a price to pay. And you will pay it, my friend. 'Cause at the end of the day, she'll be happy. But I guaran-damn-tee you won't."

Mark was past the point of smiling. He could only say, "Wow."

Cal nodded and pointed at Mark. "You get it. And that's how to be happily married."

Mark laughed. "I guess third time's the charm."

"Yup. The first one's for practice. The second one, you learn you can't win. But the third one's forever, 'cause by then, you've run out of money."

SIXTEEN

Jᴇss ꜰɪɴɪsʜᴇᴅ ᴛᴡᴇᴀᴋɪɴɢ some coding for Wanda's website and updated Wanda on her progress. She'd just hit send on her text when someone knocked at the door. It didn't sound like Mark's knock, but maybe she'd heard wrong. She'd been pretty focused on work.

He'd come back—maybe it was just to talk, but that was a good sign. Maybe it was even a new beginning.

She rushed to the mirror and fluffed her hair a little then inspected herself closer. No time for makeup, but she pulled a lip balm tube from her pocket and quickly applied it to her lips. *Aren't you optimistic?*

She opened the door. "Adam!"

He wore khakis and a pale-yellow golf shirt that looked great with his sandy-blond hair. But looking at him after so many months felt like looking at a stranger.

"Jess." He gazed fondly at her for a moment. "Sorry to show up unannounced."

Jess didn't know what to think. She had moved past what had happened, relationship-wise, but the feelings of betrayal still lingered. She had let him into her life, and he'd stolen her life savings. Now she had a new life that he wasn't a part of. Jess stopped herself. She was making too much of his visit. It was probably nothing— some unfinished business or some item she'd left behind at his apartment.

"Can I come in?"

She couldn't help but feel reluctant to let him into her cottage. It felt like he was invading her life all over again. "Let's go for a walk," she finally said.

Adam's eyebrows drew together, but he didn't protest.

Conflicting emotions seemed to close in from all sides. He'd brought with him the ghosts of good memories overshadowed by the moment he had told her he'd lost all of their money. The rush of emotions was hard to process.

They arrived at the bench overlooking the cove, where Mark had found her on the day they were caught in the rain. Adam sat down. Jess hesitated, dismayed that being with Adam there would taint every good memory she had of seeing Mark there, as well as the early days in her new home that followed.

This is my life, and he doesn't belong here. The only man who belonged there with her was Mark, but she'd lost him. She forced herself to think rationally. Adam couldn't ruin her life in Applecross Cove unless she let him, and she wasn't about to do that. So she sat down and looked out at the harbor.

"I'm in a twelve-step program," Adam said.

"Good." Jess didn't know what else to say. It was good. But it didn't undo the damage he'd done. Talking about it was like being forced to step back into her old life.

Apparently taking her silence for lack of understanding, he explained, "I have a stock-trading addiction. Turns out it's a thing. I didn't know. I just knew I was stuck on a roller coaster, and I didn't know how to get off."

He might not have known, but she had. She'd seen him change. How could he not have known he had a problem before he'd ruined his life and hers? "I'm glad it's working out for you."

"I've come to ask your forgiveness."

Jess suddenly realized she was not the good person she'd always considered herself. Adam was doing the right thing, getting help, making positive changes, and apologizing. The least she could do was forgive him. It was the right thing to do, but she couldn't. She got up. "I need to walk." The truth was, she needed to run.

They walked along the boardwalk that led to the pier, and she found herself wanting to jump into the water, anything to avoid the current situation. But Mark wouldn't be there to save her. She was on her own. Wasn't that what she'd wanted?

"I know it's a lot to just spring on you like this."

"Yeah." Jess felt all the stages of grief in rapid succession—denial, anger, bargaining, depression, and acceptance. But there was one extra one that she couldn't let go of: resentment.

Adam cleared his throat. "I can't undo what I did. It was all on me. I never deserved you. Look, I don't expect you to forgive me. I know it's too much to ask." He turned away, but Jess knew he was crying.

Her own eyes moistened. From somewhere, compassion—maybe pity—welled up inside her. She couldn't kick him when he was down. He needed her forgiveness to heal and move on with his life. Then it came to her. She needed to forgive him even more to get on with her life.

"I do. I forgive you."

He turned to her, and more honest emotions passed between them than Jess had ever felt before. For Adam, it had always been about things, but at that moment, it was about them. She wasn't sure who initiated it, but the next moment, they were in each other's arms. They held on to each other, to forgiveness, and to the bittersweet sorrow of what they'd lost. But mixed with their sorrow was hope for what the future could bring.

Adam tenderly pulled away first and held on to Jess's shoulders. "You're in my heart. That will never change." He let go of her shoulders but let one hand slide down to her hand and hold on.

"I wish you all the best, Adam."

His mouth twitched at the corners as he tried to smile. "I know. Oh. Hold on." He reached into his back pocket and pulled out an envelope. "Here. It's yours."

Jess took it and looked up at him, confused.

"Open it."

She did as he asked. "Adam!" It was a check for $50,000.

"It's your part of the down payment."

"But where did you get this?"

"I filed for bankruptcy. I had to. I didn't really have a choice. The only thing I was able to keep was my home, so I sold it."

Jess was stunned.

"I'm moving back in with my parents until I get back on my feet."

Jess was sorry to hear it. "I know it can't be easy, but it'll give you a chance to regroup."

Adam brightened with optimism. "Don't feel too

sorry for me. Do you remember their house in the Hamptons?"

Oh, yes. Jess remembered the luxurious mansion. "Yeah. Not too much of a hardship, then?" No, Adam wouldn't be at a loss for creature comforts. More importantly, he would get all the help he needed.

"I'll manage."

They walked back to Jess's cottage, and she told him about her new business and how happy her life was in Applecross Cove. She left out the part about Mark.

Adam talked of his plans for the future. He couldn't work in the market anymore, but his father had mentioned having him manage one of his divisions or giving him seed money to start his own business. He wasn't quite sure what he wanted to do yet, but he had time to figure it out.

They arrived at her driveway and said their farewells. Jess watched Adam drive away. She did forgive him, and she hoped he would find his way to happiness.

SEVENTEEN

Mark finished his beer, thanked Cal for his advice, such as it was, and headed out for an afternoon of work. Wanda's house project was on hold while they waited for permits, so he had a full afternoon to devote to his yacht. The outside was done, so he focused on the interior cabin. With no rain in sight, he thought he might be able to get a coat of varnish on the interior woodwork.

Walking along the coast tended to make him philosophical. He'd always thought he was destined for a different life, but he had reconciled himself to what he'd lost. He wasn't the first person to have to take a detour. He was still strong and healthy. He had no right to complain.

He wished things had worked out with Jess. It was one more thing in his life he'd expected to be different, but he couldn't blame her, not really. He had been where she was. Although the circumstances had been far different, he knew what it was like to rebuild a life that had taken an unexpected turn. She'd once said she wished she had met him six months from now. Maybe he should have listened. She had things to work through. He, of all people, understood that. Their lives had intersected by accident. It was not meant to be. All he could do was stay out of her way and try to forget that he loved her.

The gulls called and reminded him of how good it was to be able to walk along the harbor as they soared overhead. The ocean was so vast and deep that his problems were dwarfed in its presence.

He neared home, which brought him within sight of Jess's cottage. He'd walked past it a number of times since she'd cut things off so abruptly. Sometimes he walked by it on purpose in an attempt to steel himself against his feelings for her. But what he saw at that moment made him stop and step back, concealing himself behind a large oak before the curve in the sidewalk. His first instinct was to turn and walk in the other direction, but he could not seem to make himself move.

Jess was completely enfolded in the arms of a guy. One look at that sandy-blond hair, and he knew it was Adam. And Mark was stuck there. He didn't want to tromp past them at that little moment of theirs, so he waited and watched. It was like driving by a bad car wreck. He really, deeply did not want to see this. But he couldn't look away. His stomach churned as he watched their embrace last forever. It had to stop sometime.

Jess could not have taken Adam back. Mark exhaled in disgust. What a well-dressed, entitled-looking son of a bitch Adam was. But she'd taken him back with open arms. She preferred him to Mark! After what he did to her!

But I couldn't log into my damn broker's website without her shutting me down.

Just when he'd arrived at a place where he could let Jess go and wish the best for her, this had to happen. He felt bitter and angry.

Adam got into his car and pulled out of the driveway. Mark ducked into the shadows as he drove past. Jess's footsteps crunched on the gravel as she walked back to her cottage. Mark took one last look back at the jerk driving away then walked on. Too late, he discovered that Jess had paused at her doorway and was staring at him. He wondered how long she had known he was there, but it didn't really matter. She had seen him.

So that was what rock bottom felt like—rocky and low, with some added self-loathing. None of that was really a surprise. His mind raced in search of a believable excuse, but he came up with nothing. So he braced himself and forged ahead.

"Mark?"

"I, uh... didn't want to intrude."

Jess barely nodded as her eyes fixed on his.

He wanted to say something—to ask why she was so willing to throw herself into the arms of that a-hole who had ruined her life. But instead, he said, "Have a nice day." *Have a nice day? What the frig?* He walked past her house, feeling sure that one of them would.

EVERY YEAR, Wanda threw a preseason clambake for the locals to kick off the summer tourist season. Over the years, it had grown until she'd had to move it from her home to Cal's Place. Town residents donated seafood, corn, potatoes, and everything else they might need. It was a highlight of the season that everyone looked forward to. Jess volunteered to help Wanda with preparations leading up to the event, and she was there on the morning of the big day to help set up. So was Mark.

When Jess had first made the offer to help, Wanda warned her that Mark would be there. Jess had given it some thought but eventually dismissed her apprehensions. She had to get used to that heart-sinking reaction whenever she saw him. It would only get worse with time if she didn't face him and make it feel normal. She would have to fake normal at first, but it had to get easier with time. Still, there was no point in forcing the issue. When she could avoid an awkward situation, she busied herself with tasks that did not involve Mark.

She paused at the window to admire Mark's rounded, muscular shoulders, which were on full display as he moved picnic tables into place with one of Cal's waiters.

"If it helps any, he seems as miserable as you."

Jess turned to find Wanda beside her. She gave Wanda a sad smile. "Some things just aren't meant to be."

Wanda tilted her head. "True. But maybe sometimes they are." She gave Jess a knowing look.

"Thanks, Wanda, but I wouldn't get your hopes up." While Jess appreciated the thought, Wanda didn't really know what had happened. So she couldn't know how hopeless it was.

Wanda watched Mark and the waiter return for another table. "He's my nephew, and I love him. And I think you're terrific together. I know it's none of my business, but I find that, as I get older, I don't really give a rat's ass. So I say what I think. I care for you both, and I want you to be happy."

"We will be," Jess said. "Eventually. Just not together."

Wanda gave Jess's hand a squeeze. "Well, we'll just have to see about that."

A FEW HOURS LATER, the party was in full swing. Wanda had hired a DJ, and people were dancing, including Mark. And he wasn't just dancing—he was dancing with a woman... a very pretty woman. Jess took her glass of white wine, went inside, and sat at the bar. It was closed, but that suited Jess. It was quiet and empty, except for the occasional staff member shuttling food from kitchen to table. Outside, the song ended, but Jess was content to remain at the bar, where she could indulge in self-pity.

Cal came inside and declared, "I am done with the cooking. Let the party begin!"

Jess couldn't blame him. He'd supervised an enormous clambake while making sure his staff met the guests' needs up above at the restaurant.

Cal instructed one of his staff to oversee the cleanup then take the following day off. He went behind the bar, pulled a pint of his favorite beer, took a healthy drink, then leaned on the bar and studied Jess. "You know what you need?"

Jess looked at him for a moment then raised her glass. "I've got it right here."

Cal finished his beer with impressive speed and came around to the front of the bar. "Come with me."

"Oh. No. I'm... really, I'm happy right here where I am." By the time she finished speaking, he'd dragged her outside and onto the dance floor. She thanked God that the music was lively, except she didn't have a lively dance in her. She made an effort out of politeness because Cal was Mark's friend. But as soon as the dance was over, she intended to slip away and go home. She had done her duty to help out and be part of the community effort and spirit. But now her own spirit needed attention. She was wounded and needed some time away from Mark and his pretty dance partner.

Jess spotted Wanda and mentally mapped out a route through the crowd to thank Wanda and say goodbye. Then she would fade into the afternoon shadows and walk home. No one would miss her.

As she finalized her plan, Cal hollered out, "Mark!"

Oh, great.

Mark waved. His eyes darted to Jess, then he turned back to his dance partner, the same one as before. *Lovely couple.*

To Jess's relief, the song finally ended. Now she needed to implement her plan. She took a step back, thanked Cal for cooking, and told him to have fun. Then she began her retreat.

But Cal wasn't too quick on the uptake. He tugged on Jess's wrist. "This is my favorite song!"

It was slow. *Oh, crap. What the heck? Oh, whatever.*

It was her own fault. She should have said something less ambiguous, like "I'm done dancing forever. Goodbye." But at this point, it was easier to just indulge him than it was to make an issue of it. It wasn't as though there was anything wrong with Cal. Although he did smell a little like smoke and clams at the moment, Cal was a very nice guy. He'd just had a little to drink, and after working all day, he was ready to have some fun. He deserved to. What he didn't deserve was Jess's foul mood. So she lifted her arms and assumed an overly formal ballroom dance pose. Then, out of nowhere, Mark appeared and cut in.

After smoothly swooping in between Cal and her, Mark leaned over and said, "I've seen Cal dance. I couldn't put you through that."

The song happened to be one of her favorite ballads, which just made it worse. She couldn't do this. It brought her perilously close to allowing her feelings to show. So, with every intention of excusing herself and making a hasty retreat, she glanced up and opened her mouth to say something, but the words wouldn't come. Instead, they drew closer. Mark's hand gently pressed against the small of her back, and her heart swelled. She breathed in the scent of his clothes and of him. Her heart felt as if she were suspended at the top of a roller coaster just before it headed back downward. But in that moment, nothing mattered. It was a moment apart from real life. She gave into the dream of two souls connecting in defiance of all that would keep them apart. They closed the distance between them. His cheek touched her temple. She lifted her face and lost herself in his gaze. They might have kissed, but the song ended, and someone bumped into Jess, jarring her and destroying the moment.

Another song started. Mark took Jess's hand and led her off the dance floor and onto the lawn. The sound faded to a musical blur, and strings of lights glowed like fireflies in the dim haze of evening, casting a magical glow on the world.

An awkward few moments passed before Mark spoke. "Are you happy?"

Jess took a moment to decipher the question. *Am I happy?* She wished she knew if he was being sarcastic. *How can he ask something like that sincerely?* It didn't seem like him, but so much had happened between them that neither of them was the same. She didn't know how to react, so she took the question at face value. "I'm working on it."

He nodded thoughtfully, then his mood quickly changed. "I can't say I was pleased to see you back with Adam. I thought you were smarter than that."

"You weren't pleased?" Something in the way he'd said it rubbed her the wrong way, as if he had any say in whom she hugged in her driveway. "Well, that's too bad, isn't it? It's not really about whether you're pleased or I'm happy. It's about it being none of your business."

He looked like he'd been punched in the gut. Maybe she'd overstated her case.

Mark met Jess's flare of emotion with quiet control. "I was thinking of you. I don't want you to be hurt again."

Then just leave me alone.

Mark continued. "But you're right. It's none of my business." He glanced back in the direction of the music.

Seeing him looking away, Jess said, "You'd better get back. Your dance partner will wonder where you are." The words sounded so bitter and caustic that she wished she could take them all back. Lashing out wouldn't make anything better. She'd just lowered herself in his eyes. She wasn't proud of what she'd said, but she couldn't unsay it, so she stood her ground.

Mark met her burning gaze with his cool blue eyes. "My 'dance partner' is the wife of an old school friend. He met her in college. She majored in dance."

"Well, good for her—and for you. Enjoy yourself." She turned and started to leave.

Contempt shone in his eyes, but it was his harsh tone of voice that stopped Jess in her tracks. "Her husband is confined to a wheelchair. But he knows how much she loves dancing, and he's always loved watching her dance. So a few times a year, at celebrations like this, he encourages her to dance because it makes her happy."

Jess couldn't move, let alone speak.

Mark continued, "Those two know what love is. It's unselfish and kind." He scowled at her. "But congratulations. You've just managed to make something nice seem ugly." He shook his head and walked away.

Jess watched him walk away while she caught her breath. He was right. She was a horrible person. Worse, she was a jerk. She turned and spent the walk home hating herself.

"WELL, you're right. You were kind of a jerk."

"Thanks, Maddie. I feel better already." Jess sat on

the deck and watched the clouds pass in front of the moon as echoes of music from the clambake wafted over the water.

"C'mon, Jess. Who could blame you? You were jealous."

"That doesn't exactly excuse it." She leaned her head back and stared up at the deck roof. "It just explains what brought out my worst side."

Jess heard a smile in Maddie's voice. "Aw... I think you're being a little hard on yourself."

"Oh, just ask Mark. He can straighten you out."

"Jess, come down off that limb."

"I belong up here, away from nice people."

"Don't make me call the fire department."

"Very funny."

"The last thing you need is a couple of hunky guys on your doorstep in big boots and pants with bright-red suspenders stretched over their chests."

Jess couldn't help but laugh. "I think in real life, they wear shirts and big firemen jackets."

"Wow, you really are a buzzkill."

Jess sat forward and frowned. "Maddie!"

"I'm kidding."

Jess leaned back and sighed. "I know. I'm just not."

Maddie's tone softened. "Look, let's examine this logically and assess the real damage."

Jess furrowed her brow. "Okay." But she knew Maddie couldn't see her shaking her head.

"Did you say anything mean to his dance partner?"

"No. I didn't even meet her."

"Or her husband?"

"No."

"Good. So this is just about you and Mark."

Jess had to concede. Maddie was actually making some sense. "I guess."

"By which you mean yes."

"Yes," Jess said begrudgingly.

"Okay. Now what I'm going to say is going to sound a little crazy."

"I'll try to sound shocked."

Maddie laughed. "Very funny. See? You're already feeling better."

"Oh, I wouldn't jump to conclusions."

"So the next step—and I'm serious about this."

Jess winced.

"Tell him," Maddie said.

Jess drew back, shaking her head. "Oh, I don't think—"

"Well, I do. And I think if you were honest and explained how you felt—"

"You know, the last time you told me to be honest with him, it didn't really work out all that well."

"It's not instant pudding," Maddie said.

Jess squinted. "What?"

"In real life, you can't just add water and stir and expect instant results. Some things take time."

Jess pushed back a clump of hair that kept falling into her face. "I apologized about the whole stock thing and leaving abruptly. I thought we'd be able to work through it. But he said I have trust issues, so he didn't want to bother."

"Were those his exact words?"

"No. But I'm pretty sure that's what he meant. So that was me being honest. If I go hunt him down now and tell him I trash-talked his friend because I still have the hots for him, it isn't exactly going to make for a compelling demonstration of trust."

Maddie sighed, which Jess took as defeat. "Honey, just think about it, okay?"

"All right."

"You're not going to do it, are you?" Maddie asked frankly.

"No." Jess heaved a sigh. "Okay, I'll try."

"Good."

"Maddie?"

"Yeah?"

"Thanks."

"Call me tomorrow," Maddie said. "Okay?"

"I will." Jess leaned back and sighed. Then she picked up her wine bottle and emptied it into her glass.

She held it out in front of her. "Chardonnay, you and Maddie are the best part of today."

MARK WAS PLANTED ON A STOOL, watching the dancing, when his phone vibrated in his pocket. A text from Jess popped up on the screen.

Jess: *Maddie said I should tell you the truthhhhhh.*

He squinted at the repeated letters. That was weird. Jess was the kind of person who proofread her own shopping lists, so that was way out of character for her. His gut instinct was to ignore her, but he couldn't help himself.

He thumb-typed *"Truth?"* and resisted the temptation to add the extra letters.

Jess: *I'm sorry.*

While he decided how to respond, another text appeared.

Jess: *I was a jerk, and I hate myself for being jealous.*

Jealous? He'd been so caught up in her snarky remark and how unfair it was that he hadn't considered what might've been behind it. He'd had a knee-jerk reaction and had already begun feeling guilty for being so harsh.

Mark: *Maybe we should talk about this in person. Tomorrow?*

As he pressed send, a text from Jess popped up.

Jess: *Tonight sucks. No more Mark. No more wine. The two things I love most in the world. I wonder if the liquor store's open.*

Mark's eyes widened as he realized she'd most likely been drinking.

Mark: *Jess, do NOT get into your car.*

Jess: *Mark? Oh crap, I meant that for Maddie.*

Mark: *Jess?*

When she didn't answer, Mark panicked. It seemed pretty clear from her texts that she was in no condition to drive. He took off in a run toward her cottage. It was only a two- or three-minute run, but it felt like forever. He arrived to find her car still in the driveway. That was a relief. Now that he was there, he needed to make sure she was okay and would not be driving.

When she didn't answer his knocks, he pounded and called out her name. Thinking she might be on the deck, he ran around to the back. "Jess!" But there was still no answer. He hopped over the deck rail and reached for the back door.

"Wha...?" Jess moaned as she awoke in the deck chair. She shifted her weight, knocking over a bottle, which then rolled down the deck.

Mark caught it before it rolled off the edge, and he set it upright by the wall. "Are you okay?"

Jess sat up. "Mark? Why are you here?"

"I thought you might drive to the liquor store."

"Why? Are you out of wine too?"

He exhaled and couldn't help but smile. "No. I'm just out of my mind. C'mon, up you go."

"Where are we going?"

"To bed." He pulled her up from the chair, and she stumbled and fell into his arms.

She turned to look at him. "You're pretty sure of yourself."

He pulled her arm over his shoulder and supported her with his other arm around her waist. On the way to her bedroom, he spotted Jess's keys on the counter and put them in his pocket. "You're not driving anywhere tonight."

When they reached the bedroom, she said, "I'm not the occasional-fling type. You said it yourself."

"Yeah." He set her down on the bed, pulled off her shoes, and lifted her legs onto the bed.

Jess rolled onto her side and sank into the pillow while Mark pulled the covers over her.

"But you're not a fling," she murmured. "'Cause I love you." She drifted off to sleep.

"I love you too," Mark whispered.

EIGHTEEN

Mark sat on his deck, looking out at the sea, and the sight soothed his soul. Its buoyant strength supported massive ships as they cut through its surface, then refilled their wake until no sign remained of their presence. If only his life could be as adaptable and undaunted. But people passed through others' lives and sometimes left changes that could not be undone or forgotten.

He picked up his phone. It was nearly noon, and his text message remained unanswered. When he arrived home the previous night, he'd texted Jess. *"I've got your keys. Safety precaution."* If she hadn't responded, it had to mean she needed sleep more than she needed her keys.

He set down his phone, leaned back in his chair, and wondered what he was doing. He'd told Jess he loved her. She was asleep when he'd said it, so she hadn't heard it, but saying it out loud had made it real. He'd been hiding from it, but he couldn't deny it was the truth. Maybe admitting his feelings was the first step toward recovery.

The next truth was that he couldn't have her. She was with Adam. If she hadn't made that clear, seeing her arms wrapped around him had driven home the point. She had never denied it, so giving her any more of his heart would be an exercise in futility. It was time to move on, man up, and quit moping.

At least he'd gotten out of this thing with Jess soon enough to avoid a repeat of what had happened the last time. His marriage to Nicole had been destined for failure. If only he'd known it at the time.

NICOLE HAD COME through the accident with barely a scratch, but Mark had been seated next to the door, so he'd taken more of the impact than anyone else. Nicole was there for him in the hospital and stayed by his side until he recovered from the shoulder replacement. Before the surgery, his doctor had told him he would never swim competitively again, so there were two things to recover from, really. But Nicole went on as though Mark would prove all the doctors wrong.

He would never forget the last time she'd driven him to the pool. He had, as far as the doctors were concerned, recovered from the surgery. While he might increase his strength, his shoulder was as good as it was going to get. He couldn't even do a full lap. Even if he were able to work up to it, his shoulder would never be the same. The doctors had warned him before the surgery and had restated it after. Mark got it, but Nicole just wouldn't hear it.

As they drove home from the pool, he knew Nicole sensed something was wrong. They didn't speak the whole way home.

After they got out of the car and walked through the door, Mark stopped. "It's over."

"Swimming?"

"Us." It hurt him to have to spell it out for her.

"It's only over if you quit." She lifted her chin and stared at him with all the steely will of someone who knew nothing of how much he wanted it.

"Nicole, the doctors told me. I didn't want to believe them, but it's just not the same, and I can't will it back."

She shook her head. "You just need to train more. I'll schedule more time at the pool." She reached for her phone.

"No!" He grabbed the phone and threw it on the floor. Then he gripped her shoulders. "My stroke is gone, and it's not coming back! The Olympics are never going to happen!"

That was when he hit the bottom. He'd already lost his Olympic dream. Now he was losing his wife. She had fallen in love with a champion swimmer, and he was no longer that man. The next morning, Nicole packed a bag and moved out.

After the Olympics, she'd married one of the medalists. They divorced a year after the guy cheated on her.

THE DOORBELL RANG. Mark knew it would be Jess, there to pick up her keys, but he didn't know how miserable she would look. He chalked it up to a hangover and invited her in. He had her keys ready on the hall table. "I hope you don't mind that I took them. I just thought it would be safer."

She took the keys and averted her eyes. "I understand. Thank you."

"No problem."

She made no sign of leaving. "I'm sorry you had to see me like that."

"No worries." He took in the sight of her straight brown hair, uncombed and pulled back into a haphazard knot. She was wearing no makeup on that beautiful satin skin, which felt as soft as it looked.

They'd spent so much time stumbling over each other's feelings, yet all he wanted was to take her into his arms and kiss her and hold her. He knew she felt something. She'd told him she loved him.

But she'd obviously told Adam she loved him as well. Adam, her ex—or maybe her fiancé again. *Talk about things that make zero sense.*

Jess couldn't seem to meet his gaze. "I'm not like that. I don't usually drink, at least not like that." Her eyes finally settled on his. "I guess I don't want you to judge me."

That touched a raw nerve. "Yeah, that would feel awful to have someone see something once and then judge you—like a stock-trading website, or a dance." As bitter as he sounded, he'd actually held back so much more.

Her eyes widened, and she protested, "I didn't judge you."

"Yeah, right. Wrong choice of words. You dumped me. No, that's not quite right. You told me you loved me then dumped me."

"I'm sorry. I was afraid to fall into another stock-trading situation. And last night, well, you know. I reread my texts. I was jealous."

A host of thoughts came to the fore, and he struggled to choose the right words. But he was so clouded by anger, he knew anything he said would be brutal. So he clenched his jaw and measured his words. For someone who didn't want to fall into another stock-trading situation, she'd managed to walk back into the first one. That showed where her heart was, and it wasn't with Mark. *So what's the point anymore?* There was nothing worth saying.

Mark calmed down enough to say, "What's done is done." He wanted to say they could try to move forward together, but it was too late. She'd chosen Adam.

Jess looked as though the wind had been knocked out of her, but she recovered enough to softly say, "Thanks for the keys." And she left.

MARK HAD ALWAYS RELIED on the sea's timeless expanse to put things into perspective. But it wouldn't work this time, not where love was concerned. In the days that followed, love loomed with all of its problems. No matter how much time he spent working on Wanda's house project and his boat or talking to friends at Cal's Place, the ache was still there. His feelings for Jess overshadowed his thoughts.

THE HOURS JESS spent on her deck, phone in hand, only left advice floating around in her head, never reaching her heart. In their own ways, Mark and Jess had arrived at the same conclusion. Love wasn't always enough.

Jess pushed her chair back from her keyboard and answered the door.

"Adam."

Days had passed since she'd last spoken with Adam. She'd finally managed to leave thoughts of him firmly in her past. He was dressed in expensive casual wear and sunglasses that made him look like a movie star. This was the Adam she'd fallen in love with, radiating an exuberance that drew people to him. She was once one of those people.

Adam stepped aside and motioned proudly toward the driveway. "It's yours."

A driver secured the bed of his tow truck and pulled out of the driveway, leaving a tomato-red convertible sports car. Jess stared at the car then studied Adam through narrowed eyes. "You're trading again."

"Before you say anything, it was a one-shot deal. I had money from the sale of my condo, and there was this smoking-hot IPO that I couldn't pass up. And it paid off big."

Jess felt sick.

Adam took hold of her shoulders. "This changes everything. We can get married, just like we planned."

"No."

"I know. I know what you're thinking."

"No. That's what I'm thinking. Go home. Go to a meeting. Get some help. And for God's sake, send someone to pick up that car."

His obvious disappointment was painful to see. "Jess, I love you."

"I'm sorry, Adam. We can't be together. It's over." She ached as disappointment dulled the light in his eyes, but she had to step back and gently close the door on him and that part of her life.

MARK RUSHED to the car to help Wanda carry the cushions she'd sewn for the yacht. As they headed down the steep path to the boat, Wanda looked over at Jess's driveway. "Is that Jess's fancy new car?"

Mark grunted. "Yeah, I guess." It had been there for two days with no sign of a visitor. Jess didn't have that kind of money, so it had to be from Adam. *How nice for her.*

Wanda stopped at the bottom of the hill and took in the sight. "It's gorgeous! Mark, look what you've done!"

He banished thoughts of Jess and smiled broadly.

Wanda got misty-eyed. "Your grandfather would have been so proud of you! Wait 'til your parents see it. Oh! You could sail down to Florida!"

"The hull needs to be rebuilt before I take an ambitious trip like that. Besides, you keep me pretty busy here." With a wave, he said, "Come on. Let me give you the grand tour."

He showed her around the deck and pointed out his favorite features, then they went into the cabin. Mark put the cushions in place, and Wanda was thrilled to see that they fit. She sat down, still smiling.

"It's comfortable!" Mark sat across from her, stretched out his arms, and let his gaze sweep through the cabin. "This is the first time I've just sat here, relaxing. It feels good."

"You deserve it."

They sat and chatted about the yacht and the progress on the house renovation. Then Wanda broached the topic of Jess.

Mark shook his head. "It just never worked. I wanted it to, but I don't know." He shrugged helplessly.

Wanda's eyes brightened. "This yacht calls for a

celebration. I wouldn't dream of breaking a bottle on your gorgeous woodwork, but I'll buy you one to share over lunch."

"Sounds perfect." He offered a steadying hand as she climbed from the cabin and onto the dock. Then he secured the cover, and they headed up the steep hill as they discussed which seafood place to go to.

THE TOW TRUCK came and took away the little red sports car, much to Jess's relief. She couldn't help feeling like Adam had invaded her space, bringing back all the frustration and sorrow. She loved him still, in a way, but that way was too painful and no longer the sort of love she could build her life on.

Having worked two weeks straight, Jess took the day off. The wind had picked up, so she pulled on a jacket and headed out for a walk by the harbor. She got a haddock sandwich from a dockside stand and found a picnic table with a view of the boats. Since she'd moved there, she'd never been out on a boat. She decided today was the day, so she went to a stand to reserve a spot on the next sightseeing yacht going out.

"Sorry," the man said. "A storm's coming in. There's a lightning-storm warning, so we're not going out."

"Oh, okay. Some other time." Jess was a bit disappointed, but it wasn't like there wouldn't be other chances. After all, she only lived a short walk away.

Instead, she stopped at some shops, treated herself to a scented candle, a half-pound of Jamaican Blue Mountain coffee, and a small box of fudge that she swore she would ration out sensibly. *Right.* Her last stop was another seafood stand for some fish and chips to take home for dinner.

The wind whipped strands of hair against her face as she made her way home. By the time she walked up to her door, dark clouds had made the afternoon sky look like evening. She made it inside and checked the weather report on her phone. They'd told her at the yacht stand that a storm was blowing in, but she hadn't realized how severe it might be. She took another look out the window and was glad to be inside and safe. It was still her day off, so she decided to enjoy it by curling up with a good book. A loud noise outside sent her out to the deck, where a tree branch had broken off and struck the back of the cottage. No damage was done, but she decided to move the deck furniture close to the house to lessen the chances of it being tossed by the wind. Once that was done, she started to head inside when she caught sight of the small potted plant Mark had given her. It was tipped on its side, so she brushed the spilled soil back into the pot and brought it inside with her. The wind caught the door, but she won the struggle to close it.

Once inside, Jess stared at the pot. "Maybe I should've let the wind have its way with you." But in the midst of the soil was a tiny sprout. "Well, look at you." She picked up the pot and examined the bud closer. It wore a broken sunflower seed like a hat and was bright green and thriving. Unexpected delight sprang up from within. Mark would be pleased.

But her joy instantly faded. He wouldn't see or care about the plant he had given her because he wouldn't see or care about her. She set the sprout down on the windowsill where it would get enough sun, then she poured a few tablespoons of water into the clay pot.

Jess glanced out the window and caught sight of Mark's boat. She knew he was on the boat, tying down loose bits of canvas. She grimaced. She had to stop looking over there. But the only way she could avoid it would be to cover the windows and never look out, which defeated the purpose of living somewhere so beautiful. She would just have to get used to viewing him as if he were just another part of the landscape—a landscape with broad shoulders and thick, tousled hair.

A blinding flash and deafening crack made her jump as a lightning bolt struck the mast of Mark's boat. Panic shot through her. She had just seen him down there. She bolted out the door then took off running down the pathway and stairs to the dock.

"Mark!" The canvas cover was unfastened partway and flapping in the wild wind, so she climbed onboard and went into the cabin. "Mark!" It was empty, so she climbed back out into the pelting rain. Thunder cracked nearby. She was terrified, but not finding Mark scared her more. She called out twice more but got no answer.

Mark wasn't on the boat or the dock. Jess shuddered when she realized he must be in the water. Storm clouds darkened the sky, and pelting rain made it nearly impossible to see, but she had no choice but to try to find him.

Jess kicked off her shoes and plunged into the water. She swam around one side of the dock, where he might have fallen, waving her arms about and relying on touch more than sight. She'd never practiced swimming underwater, but she took a deep breath and dove down again. Unable to see very much through the dark, stinging salt water, she grasped through the water in hopes of finding him. She emerged with a splash and called out again then swam under the dock to continue her search. She was frantic. What if he was unconscious down there? How long could he survive? She dove back underwater, blindly reaching about, losing hope, but pressing on with her search.

With her lungs ready to burst, she shot up to the surface and gasped. A strong arm hooked under her arm and guided her by the chin to the ladder at the end of the dock then pushed her up the ladder. She climbed out, and Mark followed behind her then pulled her against him.

They clung to each other, then Mark took her face in his hands. "Are you okay?"

She nodded. "I saw you down here, and then lightning struck."

"I'm okay. Come on. We've got to get out of this storm."

Lightning flashed, and thunder boomed the next second. Mark took Jess's hand, and together, they ran up the steps and along the path to Mark's house. Inside, Mark pulled her into his embrace and held her. Then he kissed her forehead and pulled her back into his arms.

"You're shivering." He led her to a chair. "Wait right there."

Still catching her breath, Jess had no intention of going anywhere. Mark returned with towels and a blanket. He wrapped the blanket around her and dried her hair with the towel. Then he dried himself off and set about starting a fire. When he had a good fire blazing, he brought a chair close to hers, and they huddled together for warmth. But as they began to relax by the fire, their huddled embrace changed. Jess lifted her chin and looked into his eyes. Mark leaned over and kissed her until she felt weak and lightheaded. His kiss grew more urgent as his hands slid down to her shoulders.

Abruptly, he stopped and leaned back. "I'm sorry." He exhaled. "I had no right to do that."

"Mark—"

He put distance between them. "It was stupid. I know you're with Adam."

Jess was stunned. "Adam?" Confusion rendered her speechless for a moment. Finally, she managed to ask, "Where did you get that idea?"

"I saw him over there... with you."

"Doing what?" She couldn't believe what she was hearing. "Hugging goodbye? Because that's all you could have seen."

Mark was slack-jawed.

"I haven't been with Adam since I moved here. You know that."

"But the red car—"

"Is gone. So is Adam. He's trading again, and it's over. I'm over him." She stopped. An odd calm draped itself over her as she searched Mark's eyes. "You kissed me," she said softly.

"Because I love you," he said simply.

A rush of emotion filled Jess's heart so much it

ached. "I shouldn't have let anything come between us."

"I'll get a stockbroker to manage my investments."

Jess shook her head. "I was scared of all the wrong things, and the ones that were right, I just made a mess of." She exhaled. "I love you." She got up and threw her arms about Mark's neck.

He held her and kissed her forehead and hair. "That's all behind us."

Jess gazed into his eyes. "Could we start over again?"

"No."

Before she could voice her surprise, he said, "Let's pick up where we left off after the wedding. I never finished giving you the grand tour. My bedroom's pretty amazing." He smiled. "There's a steam shower up there."

Still wearing her wet, sea-soaked clothes, Jess sighed. "A steam shower sounds so good."

"It works better with two." He took her hand. "Come with me." And he led her upstairs.

NINETEEN

THE MORNING WAS sunny and calm, as if the storm had never happened. Mark handed Jess a mug of hot coffee, and they curled up together on the sofa, facing the wall of windows that looked out to the cove.

"I saw you on the boat," Jess said.

"Stalking me, were you?"

She recoiled. "No!" *Maybe.* "It's not my fault. My kitchen window just happens to face your direction. I've been meaning to order some blackout curtains." She made a face, and he laughed.

The spark in her eyes faded. "A minute later, I turned back and saw lightning strike. I've never been that close. Then I realized you were gone."

"Well, you're right. I was on the boat. And I'm not gonna lie. It shook the whole boat. Scared the sh— sorry, body contents—out of me. I mean not literally."

Jess grimaced. "Ew."

"Anyway, so it hit, and—"

Jess was still in stunned disbelief. "How could you survive something like that?"

"The boat's fitted with a lightning protection system, which must have minimized the damage. After my ears stopped ringing, I made a mad dash for the house."

"I ran out there as soon as I saw the lightning."

Mark peered at her soberly. "Most people run away from lightning, not toward it. Don't do that again."

Jess's eyes stung. "I couldn't just leave you there."

"But I wasn't there, was I?"

"You must have been halfway up the hill by the time I ran out of the house."

Mark drew her closer into his embrace. "I reached the first landing, and I heard you shouting. I hollered back, but you obviously didn't hear me. I ran down to you, but by the time I got there, you'd jumped into the water. By the way, what were you thinking?"

"You weren't in the cabin, so I figured you must have fallen into the water. You could have been injured or slipped and fallen. I didn't know, but I was sure you were in trouble."

"You gave me a scare," Mark said. "I couldn't find you at first. I was sure you were drowning. I taught you some basics, but you're in no way prepared to maneuver in that rough water."

Proudly, Jess lifted her chin. "I've been practicing. I can swim laps."

"Rescuing someone is not quite as easy."

She looked into his eyes. "I didn't have a choice." Her eyebrows drew together as she turned away. "Except you weren't there. You didn't need to be rescued."

Mark's eyes sparkled. "Don't feel bad. I rescued a woman who wasn't actually drowning."

Jess gazed into the fire. "It was like the swim of the Magi."

Mark smirked. "Yeah, something like that." He took her face in his hands and planted a kiss on her lips that took their minds off the storm and more or less everything else but each other.

TWENTY

THAT AFTERNOON, someone came out to assess the lightning damage. Mark was relieved to learn that the yacht had survived nearly unscathed except for the electronics. If that was the worst, he could live with it.

They had to wait a few days to get the new radio installed. But the time finally came to take the yacht out for her maiden voyage.

Jess arrived, beaming, and presented Mark with her sunflower sprout. With a ceremonious air, she said, "Look what survived being with me!"

"Congratulations," Mark said. Her proud look was endearing.

Jess eagerly asked, "Does it look like it's ready to be transplanted?"

"As soon as we get back." He flashed a smile and set it on one of the steps.

"You won't step on it, will you?"

He laughed. "Promise."

Wanda arrived with a picnic lunch. It had been her father's boat, after all, so it was important to Mark that she be there for the first outing. Since she had brought Jess and Mark together in the first place, it felt like a family outing of sorts.

Wanda pulled a bottle of champagne from her bag. "For later."

"Perfect!" Mark said.

Wanda cheerfully said, "I'll just put this on ice."

"Ice?"

"Don't worry. I brought some."

Mark held out his hand to offer support as she boarded the yacht. Once there, she turned. "Wait! What's her name? New boat, new name."

Mark's face went blank. "I haven't thought about that." He looked at Jess, and his lips spread into a smile. "The *Sunflower*."

Wanda had sailed all her life, so with Mark at the helm, she served as first mate.

"Now, Jess, pay attention. Who knows? You might want to go sailing with Mark on your own." She talked Jess through everything she was doing, enlisting Jess's help when she could.

GLINTS OF LIGHT sparkled on the surface of the water as they chose a scenic spot near the shore to furl the sails and drop anchor. Wanda brought out the champagne and put it in a bucket of ice while Jess retrieved the sandwiches Wanda had packed. When they were ready to eat, Jess asked, " Shall we open the champagne?"

Wanda drew her eyebrows together. "It needs to chill a bit first."

Jess eyed the condensation that clung to the bottle but said nothing.

They proceeded with lunch. When Jess wasn't looking, Mark cast a knowing look at Wanda and winked.

"You know, Mark, I'm not as agile as I used to be," Wanda said. "I'm afraid you'll have to find a new first mate to take over my duties."

Mark nodded. "I have someone in mind. She's a good learner. Picked up swimming quickly enough." He gazed at Jess, who smiled back. His eyebrows drew together. "It's a long-term position, though—permanent, really. So she might not be amenable to the job duties and terms."

Jess stared at her sandwich. "She might not be looking for a boss." She cast a doubtful look at Wanda, who only grinned back.

Jess took a bite of her sandwich.

Mark nodded emphatically. "Oh, it would be an equal partnership."

Wanda watched Jess's expression transform as she appeared to catch on that Mark was no longer kidding. Nor was he talking just about sailing.

Jess set down her sandwich and wiped her face and hands with her napkin then anchored it under her plate. "Mark?"

Mark's eyes dimmed. "Do you think she'd say yes?"

Wanda had never seen Mark look so nervous.

"I think you should ask her," Jess said softly.

Mark got down on one knee before her. "Would you—"

"Yes!"

"—marry me?"

"Yes!"

Wanda popped the cork while Jess threw her arms about Mark.

ACKNOWLEDGMENTS

Editing by Red Adept Editing
redadeptediting.com

THANK YOU!

Thank you, reader. With so many options, I appreciate your choosing my book to read. Your opinion matters, so please consider sharing a review to help other readers.

BOOK NEWS

Would you like to know when the next book comes out? Click below to sign up for the J.L. Jarvis Journal and get book news, free books, and exclusive content delivered monthly.

news.jljarvis.com

ABOUT THE AUTHOR

J.L. Jarvis is a left-handed opera singer/teacher/lawyer who writes books. She received her undergraduate training from the University of Illinois at Urbana-Champaign and a doctorate from the University of Houston. She now lives and writes in upstate New York.

Sign up to be notified of book releases and related news:
news.jljarvis.com

Email JL at:
writer@jljarvis.com

Follow JL online at:
jljarvis.com

facebook.com/jljarvis1writer

twitter.com/JLJarvis_writer

instagram.com/jljarvis.writer

bookbub.com/authors/j-l-jarvis

pinterest.com/jljarviswriter

goodreads.com/5106618.J_L_Jarvis

amazon.com/author/B005G0M2Z0

youtube.com/UC7kodjlaG-VcSZWhuYUUl_Q